UNTIL YOU COME HOME

UNTIL YOU COME HOME

The Endless Wait for a Beloved to Come Home from War

MRIDULA BAJPAI

AMARYLLIS

AMARYLLIS

An imprint of Manjul Publishing House Pvt. Ltd.
• 7/32, Ansari Road, Daryaganj, New Delhi 110 002
Website: www.manjulindia.com
Registered Office:
10, Nishat Colony, Bhopal 462 003 - India

Untill You Come Home by Mridula Bajpai

ISBN 978-93-87383-20-3

This edition first published in 2018

Printed and bound in India by
Thomson Press (India) Ltd.

Dedication

To Captain K L Shukla and
all the brave men who laid down
their lives while defending
the Se-La Pass, in November 1962

From the core of my heart...

For me, writing this story was akin to performing a *yajna*, for which I had to offer a part of myself with each *aahuti*. Only then did this story take it's present form.

A lot of people have contributed directly or indirectly in the telling of this story. I am grateful to all of them.

First and foremost, I thank my sister, Dr. Meenakshi Bajpai, who made me aware of the writer inside me.

My mother, and my daughter, sweet Chini gave me unstinted support and strength during the writing of this novel. They put up with my late night writing sessions, and sacrificed time which was theirs.

I do not find adequate words in any dictionary that would suffice to thank all my friends in the Indian Army for their support and encouragement.

I thank my husband, Devendra, who's my friend and also my worst critic, for supporting me throughout the writing of this novel. Being an Army Officer, the suggestions he gave were of invaluable help.

I'd also like to thank Vikas Rakheja, my publisher, for his faith in me, and for publishing this novel.

I am indebted to my friend and editor, Manoj Kulkarni, who was associated with the writing of this novel from the very beginning. He read and re-read the manuscript and gave useful suggestions.

I thank Abraham Varghese, who typeset the manuscript meticulously.

This is not just Neeraja, Captain Uday Sharma and Jaya's; Major Dev Sharma and Mrinalini's, or Shubha and Manu's story. It may very well be yours or that of someone you know. Be it Jaya's agony and torment or Neeraja's endless wait for her brother Uday to come back home from war, or Dev's infinite love for Mrinalini, or Shubha's love for little Manu, which is greater than that of a mother for her own child.

Everything in the story appears very real and familiar. I'm sure you may have come across many such characters in your life. You may feel that this has happened to you or to someone around you, and will identify with many of these characters and feel an intangible, yet very real bond with them.

I take this opportunity to remember my mama, Captain K L Shukla of 4 Sikh Light Infantry, who laid down his life in defense of the Se-La Pass in November 1962. I have known the agony and torment that a *fauji's* family goes through when he does not come home from war. Still, the family lives in hope, waiting and forever chanting in their hearts... 'we are waiting – *until you come home...*'

1

I don't remember how many people I must have met in my life, or when I parted ways with them. But as I have never ever met Uday mama, our ways never really parted. Therefore, as such, in every moment of my life, Uday mama has remained with us. It is as if I have lived longer with him than I have with myself.

Mummy had her own special ways of remembering Uday mama. Right from the very beginning, she missed him. She would say little, but sometimes on *Raakhi*, we saw her surreptitiously wiping away her tears. Sometimes, we would see her awake late in the night, quietly turning over pages of the old family album. She would often read and re-read old letters, and sometimes, she would quietly call out to him.

I still remember that old trunk in our house. In my childhood, I thought it contained only old, forgotten knick-knacks, or was used to put away *razais* after the winters. Twice a year, mummy would very religiously open the trunk, once at the onset of winters and again at the advent of summers – all the old stuff would be pulled out to be dusted and dried in the sun, only to be put away once again.

That year, as the winters approached once again – I must have been in Class XI – one evening, mummy was busy taking out all the old stuff from the trunk and putting it back carefully. I noticed, for the very first time, an olive green raincoat being taken out. The same type as used by the Army. Mummy carefully took it out and touching it affectionately, hid her face in it. She was crying. When she raised her face, I noticed her moist eyes. She ignored my presence and continued with her work. It was obvious that the raincoat was Uday mama's.

Later on, at some point, she did mention, "Uday had come to Sagar in July 1960 and had forgotten to take back his raincoat." This raincoat has always been a part of my existence ever since. As the years went by the raincoat became increasingly old and tattered, but Uday mama always remained with us.

Captain Uday Sharma was posted in the NEFA* during the Chinese aggression of 1962. The Indian Army fought a fierce battle at the NEFA to save the Se-La Pass in November that year. Uday mama's Battalion suffered heavy losses in the war. Ten of the thirteen officers never returned home.

Since childhood, I had been hearing my nana say, "More than half the Unit is still listed as missing in action." Perhaps mummy is still waiting for Uday mama to come home. Even today, mummy hopes to see her brother return, some day.

"My eyes search forever, far into the distance, awaiting Uday's return. How many people have since gone – your nana, your papa and amma. Amma had already gone. May be it was for the best, else would she have been able to bear this sorrow of losing her only son?"

---

* The North-East Frontier Province

To this day, mummy remembers every single moment of that fateful night. It's as clear as a movie playing before her eyes. It had been a bitterly cold night. Everyone was having a cup of tea after dinner. Nana was relaxing on the easy chair in front of the fireplace. There was a certain, unfathomable heaviness in the atmosphere. All of them were pretending that there was nothing unusual, but there was absolute silence, as though there was an unknown, unseen but very perceptible fear lurking around.

It had been a few weeks since Uday and his Unit had left for the NEFA. The effort being made to appear normal was making the entire evening look all the more abnormal. On that dark, cold and quiet night, when all the windows and doors were shut tight, a gust of breeze entered as if from nowhere and Uday mama's photograph kept on top of the fireplace fell to the ground and was shattered to pieces. Mummy even now remembers Uday mama's smiling face amidst the pieces of broken glass, against the brightness of the flames in the fireplace. Nana was convinced right then that something terrible had happened to his son.

Nana would keep awake night after night, smoking one cigarette after another. Everyone remained tense. He would tell Bahadur, "Don't lock the main gate. Uday might come anytime."

Mummy keeps recalling those days every now and then. It is as if those days have never gone away. How strange and full of tension those days must have been.

Uday mama has not come back home. Everyone misses him and still awaits his return. Mummy and nana would feel this intense pain and tried hard to hide it from each other, though unsuccessfully. They would pretend everything was fine. Mummy would never show her pain even to papa. She always battled with this sorrow alone.

"Poor Jaya, she could not even show her pain openly, for no tangible relationship existed now between her and Uday." Mummy would often remember Jaya saying this. Mummy would then be all alone with her pain, quietly, for days to come.

Whenever she would mention Uday mama, Jaya's name would effortlessly come up in her conversation.

Seeing mummy's stoic silence, I would think of the immense pain that she was going through. She had probably visited all temples, *dargahs* and other places of worship she could, and had prayed and pleaded for her brother's safe return. The countless threads of *mannat* that she had tied at a thousand places remained as they were. They must still be tied in the same places, even today. Time would definitely have faded the colours of those threads, but they would still be there. Wouldn't the knots of *mannat* have become loose with time? Why had desperate prayers gone unheard and unanswered? Mummy's faith and belief are still firm. But had Uday mama forgotten to keep his promises that he had made to everyone?

Will anyone have answers to any of these questions?

I still remember nana saying to himself in an emotional moment to himself, "Would it have been easy to reach Se-La Pass? It was at a height of 14000 feet, covered with snow. Our Army did not have adequate warm clothing to beat the bitter cold. Neither did they have enough ammunition and wherewithal. Everything was so sudden and unexpected. There was confusion all around. No one knew anything for certain. The Indian Army was probably not at all prepared for the war. It was in these extremely tough conditions that my Uday had fought," saying this he would, as always, become silent and gaze into oblivion, far out of the window.

Nana, till his last breath, had waited for his son to come back home.

2

Since childhood, Shubha and I used to hear a lot about Uday mama. Nana used to say, "I was very keen to join the Army, but my family did not let me. So, the day Uday was born, I decided I will make him an Army Officer. We already had a lot of land and property. Your nani was reluctant to let her only son join the Army, but as soon as Uday turned eleven, I got him admitted to the Prince of Wales Military College* in Dehradun."

In order to fulfill his dreams, nana got Uday mama admitted to the best institution. "My son fulfilled the tradition of the Army, he fought till the end and went down fighting," nana would remember with tear-filled eyes.

His son had laid down his life fighting to his last breath. His son's sacrifice was a reality that nana knew, but never could come to terms with.

Uday mama's childhood memories had become a frequent part of our conversations at home.

Mummy would affectionately remember, "Our Uday

---

* Now called the Rashtriya Indian Military College (RIMC).

was very naughty." It would seem little Uday had come back to her once again.

"Mr Catchpole, an Englishman, was the principal of Uday's school in Dehradun. He grew nice, juicy tomatoes in his garden. Uday, in all his naughtiness, had plucked and thrown around more tomatoes than he had eaten. In the darkness of the night, he had also managed to uproot many of the plants and had even got caned for it the next day. When he came home after three weeks, marks of the caning could still be seen clearly."

Nana would continue, "When Uday was leaving Dehradun to join the National Defense Academy at Khadakvasla, Mr Catchpole came to the station, and giving him a big box said, "Open it only once the train leaves." When Uday opened the box, it was full of tomatoes… ripe, red tomatoes, and also delicious sandwiches made by Mrs Catchpole! Uday was instantly reminded of the caning."

To this day, a name remains entwined with Uday's – that of Jaya. Whenever Uday is spoken of, Jaya's name comes up naturally. When Shubha and I were growing up, we would often hear Uday mama and Jaya being mentioned together, so we automatically developed an attachment towards their relationship. We would talk about them for long hours. We would forever be curious to know, discover and understand their love.

We had heard from mummy that whenever Uday mama came on vacation from school, all arrangements would be made by Jaya's father, Colonel Mishra. Actually, mama would come home only after meeting Jaya in Lucknow. By and by, Shubha and I started understanding this beautiful relationship.

"Whenever Uday would help Jaya with her studies, she would be least interested," I once told Shubha.

"Jaya would often write her name on Uday's palm, hardly paying any attention to studies," Shubha would tell with mock seriousness.

"Jaya once knit a sweater for Uday. Only I know how she did it as she did not know anything about knitting," mummy had once said.

Jaya, as she grew up, always dreamt of a life with Uday, carrying his image in her heart. By the time she finished school, she had begun to dream about her marriage.

"Whenever Uday came on leave to Lucknow, he and Jaya would roam around the Residency, the Imambara and other places. They took hundreds of pictures together." Once while climbing the steps of the Bhul-bhulaiya, Jaya became breathless, "I can't climb anymore, Uday. I am nearly dead. It's almost as if you are taking me on a route-march," she had said. Uday had then helped her climb.

"Jaya, I will always be with you. You have become tired while climbing only these many steps?... We have a long way to go together."

When they reached the terrace of the Bhul-bhulaiya, the floor was very hot and Jaya's feet started to burn. She put her delicate feet on Uday's and said, "My feet are burning." Then, joking, she said, "Let me see how much you love me. For how long can you stand like this on this scaldingly hot floor? My feet don't hurt anymore!"

Uday had stood on silently for ten minutes. She was very happy that Uday, out of his love, was keeping his feet on the hot floor. When she tried to remove her feet, Uday had stopped her and said, "Keeping your feet on mine was your decision, but removing them is not. You think that I am such a weakling? I can keep you comfortable for much longer than ten minutes. God knows I could stand like this till I perished."

Only after Jaya had said sorry and started crying, had Uday let her remove her feet. He had then teased her a lot, "At the National Defense Academy we would be punished... and would be made to do countless front-rolls, shirtless in the hot sun. These are a *fauji's* feet, not the delicate feet of a *fauji's* wife!"

Nana and mummy often remembered Uday mama's Passing Out Parade at the Indian Military Academy. Nana, mummy, Col Mishra and Jaya went for the grand event. It was December of 1957. It was cold, but pleasantly sunny. Jaya's happiness could not be missed. She appeared overwhelmed. Jaya and Uday went around Dehradun. Jaya also visited Uday's school, PWMC (now RIMC).

"Tell me, Uday, where all have you done front-rolls? How many canings and punishments did you get while you were there? Which was your room? Where all did you think of me – under this tree? Or was it on the grass over there?" Jaya had asked innumerable questions.

Uday had lived here from 1948-1953, and walking through those corridors, Jaya's happiness knew no bounds. Then, on a serious note, she said, "You have been posted to Assam. Daddy will think of our marriage only when you get posted to a peace station."

On hearing this, nana said to the Col Mishra, "Your daughter no long wants to stay in Lucknow with you. Jaya, after marriage, stay with us. Uday's posting does not matter."

Mummy had mentioned that Jaya was very fond of bangles, so much so that when she was in Dehradun for Uday's Passing Out Parade, she had managed to find a bangle shop. "I will wear at least two dozen bangles today and that too, the most expensive ones that I can find," she had said affectionately to Uday.

"Jaya, wear red bangles, lots of them. *Faujis* anyway are not rich people. It's great that you are happy with glass bangles," Uday had teased.

Whenever Uday mama came on leave, Jaya would always visit a bangle shop with him. As soon as he arrived, she would say, "Uday, let's go to the *churiwaala* and buy lots of *churis*."

"How lucky this damn *churiwaala* is. My wife to be always wants to run to his shop. Maybe I too should set up a *churi* shop," he would say in mock anger.

"You do not even know how to put bangles on my hands. Once when we were children, my hand had started to bleed while you were slipping bangles on it. How I had cried then, seeing all that blood," Jaya would remind him.

Later, when Uday mama's belongings came back to us, we found the musical lighter that Jaya had given him when he got commissioned. It's music had touched a few moments, giving melody to them and then lost its echo. The resonance had then become silent forever. Looking at it, mummy would say, "Uday was so fond of music. Jaya had bought him this musical lighter along with a cigarette case. He was a chain smoker."

Shubha and I would talk to each other, "Jaya, out of love, would tell Uday to stop smoking."

"And do you know what he would reply?" Shubha would ask mischievously and then answer herself, "It's you who has given me this lovely lighter and the cigarette case. To what better use could I put these lips of mine while on duty than light up a cigarette."

I would add, "Do you know what Jaya might have said?"

"I'll kill you."

"I am already as good as dead," he would have replied, laughing.

We sisters had probed deep into this love story of theirs. We had, in a way, as good as done a complete thesis on it! Our sources were as diverse and varied as the conversations between papa and mummy, the old maid at home, and a lot of stories from Bahadur's wife, Maya.

We had also managed to gather a lot of detailed information about the war. Since early childhood, we had heard that a war-like situation had emerged at the border with China by the time it was September, 1962. A lot of rumours were floating around. By October, the Chinese had occupied Tawang. Heavy movement of the Army had started. A lot of Units had moved forward, with many of them being sent towards the NEFA.

At home everyone was relieved that Uday's Unit had come back from Goa just the year before. Therefore, they were unlikely to be mobilized, still everyone was tense.

Jaya too would be very worried. She would try and console herself. When she would become very anxious she would ask her father, "Daddy, Uday's Unit has just returned after liberating Goa, they should not be mobilised."

"Yes they should stay put at the peace station," Col Mishra would reassure his daughter, though tense himself.

Everybody thought that after liberating Goa, Uday's Unit would remain at the peace station. Who knew then that they would be sent to the treacherous mountains of the North-East so soon. Who would have thought that the Chinese, after chanting *"Hindi Chini Bhai Bhai,"* would betray the Indians so quickly. On 20th October 1962, all the Officers of Uday's Unit had gathered in the Officers' Mess. It had been Lt Sanjeev Singh's birthday. Rumours were rife that everyone would be moved and the orders could be received any moment. On the occasion of parties, such talks never surfaced. At that very moment, that confidential message from the Brigade Headquarters had arrived, the "order to move", and what an express order to move it was...

The entire Unit had to move within 48 hours. For a moment, silence fell and then there was loud rapture and merry-making. Everyone was very keen to celebrate as much as they could, before moving. One last time, as for many, it would prove to be the last party they would ever have. By the time the party got over, there was chaos and confusion everywhere.

Half the Unit left for Ambala and Agra the very next day, from where they were airlifted to Tezpur. Within 48 hours, the Army men had landed from the cool climes of Himachal to the treacherous ice-clad mountains at 14,000 feet in Arunachal. Most of them did not even have adequate warm clothing or shoes. But for the war, they would never have been sent to such heights. There had been no time for acclimatisation.

After briefing from the Commanding Officer, Col Mehta, Uday went to the Mess and sat down. Thoughts of Jaya came flooding back to him. How would he tell her of this? She was busy with preparations for the wedding and had just come back to Lucknow after shopping in Delhi. She was anxiously waiting for November.

After a lot of thinking, he decided to go to Col Mehta's house. Mrs Mehta, trying desperately to hold back her tears behind her smile, said, "So, finally, the orders have come?"

"Yes ma'am, we are going to be a part of this and will see some action."

Col Mehta remarked, "We are in high spirits. My boys have just come back from Goa."

"Have you told Jaya?" Mrs Mehta enquired.

"Not yet. Will drop a letter once I reach there," Uday replied with sadness.

"Are you crazy, Uday? Is this how you think you will tell her?" Mrs Mehta asked again.

Col Mehta said, smiling, "We could send Uday with ammunition and heavy baggage on the special train. The train will go via Lucknow. He can meet Jaya there for a short while."

The train left Ambala and reached Lucknow late at night. Col Mishra, Mrs Mishra and Jaya were waiting at the station since evening. Since it was a special train, the time of its arrival could not be ascertained.

"Daddy, do check from the enquiry," Jaya asked.

"*Beta*, it's a special train. Nobody will be able to tell us anything," Col Mishra replied.

At last the train arrived at two in the morning. Uday got down from the train. Col Mishra said, shaking Uday's hand, "So, Uday, another victory in waiting after Goa? All the best."

"*Beta*, come back soon. We will be waiting," Mrs Mishra said, putting up a brave front.

After this, Col and Mrs Mishra went and sat on a bench. Holding Uday's hand, Jaya got inside the train. There was silence for a long time. Finally, Jaya said, "Uday are you really going? Alone? Leaving me here? Come, let's get married right now."

But Uday remained silent. Jaya said lovingly, "Uday, I am in love with a Captain. Please help me out. He does not want to marry me right now. What do I do?"

When Uday still remained silent, Jaya's patience gave way. The fear of parting and the very little time in hand made her break down. She held his hand and implored, "Uday, let's get married. There is no temple or *pundit* around, but so what? If we cannot invite family and friends, let the moon, which is yet to set and the sun, which is about to rise, and the stars in the sky all be witness to our marriage."

Uday said in a trembling voice, "Jaya, if I do not come back, get married to someone else. Let the sun, the moon and the stars not be a witness to our love, for they will never let you forget me."

But Jaya kept repeating, "You will not be able to forget me. We have come a long way together, Uday, look into my eyes and you will see your image. I don't know when my heart and soul became yours."

"Don't weaken my resolve, Jaya. Look carefully into my eyes and you will see nothing. Nobody has ever been able to sail the high seas in a boat made out of paper. I have to go, Jaya. Don't stop me." By now, he had become quite forlorn.

Jaya tried desperately to persuade him in a thousand different ways, but he remained silent. At last she said, "Uday, look at me once."

"Jaya, never call out to a person who is leaving. What if I don't come back...?" He was unable to even look at Jaya.

"Don't talk of inauspicious things early in the morning. What will happen to me? Without you I will be dead. Uday, you have got to come back for me."

"Jaya, who knows what the future has in store for us?"

Hearing this, Jaya kept her head on his shoulder and started sobbing, but it was not possible to read Uday's thoughts. May be he wanted to accept what Jaya wanted, yet he knew that he might not come back. Hence, he could not even look into Jaya's eyes. If he had glanced at those eyes even for a moment, he would not be able to leave. Not listening to his own heart, he said, "Jaya, don't spoil your life. If something were to happen to me, find someone else. Forget the past and move on in life."

"Uday, let me at least come with you up to Misamari. You can travel with the convoy from there. So what if we could not walk the seven steps together, let's at least walk a few."

"Jaya, who knows what tomorrow brings? May be there is no tomorrow for us. I do not even have a today that

I can give you. You must get married if I do not come back. Promise me," he had become desperate by now.

"Uday, please listen to me now. The morning sun is about to rise. Let's get married," she tried hard to pursuade him once again.

"Let this night never end because once the day breaks, I will not be here. May be this night will not give way to any morning... for this morning will bring nothing for us."

"Uday, will you be able to bear this separation? Why are you questioning our love today? I have loved you since childhood. Please listen to me," she held on to his hand with tears in her eyes.

The train had started to move. Uday got inside the train and Jaya's hand slipped out of his.

With a firm resolve, Uday was leaving behind everything now.

Even today, Jaya must be remembering that loving, parting touch of Uday's. This feeling, this emotion would have become a part of their existence forever, for these are things which are beyond one's physical being. What is experienced by the soul, the eternal and the heart becomes a part of the sub-conscious and remains forever, even after the physical self ceases to exist.

Uday would have been haunted by so many memories as he travelled to Misamari. He would have spoken to the long and dark silence within himself. Would he ever be able to forget that lovely face? He used to tease her so much. Who knew that those loving moments when he said, "What will you do if do not come back?" would come true one day.

Jaya would remain quiet realizing that it had become a habit of Uday's to tease her. "Will you not shed even a single tear? You profess such undying love for me, cry at least a bit for Capt Uday Sharma," he would laugh loudly.

"Uday, how many times should I tell you not to say such ominous things. Promise me right now that you will not say this ever again. If you really love me, you will never repeat this," Jaya would start to cry.

"Okay, I promise, but promise me one thing in turn."

"If you will not say this, I promise to do whatever you say," she said happily.

"Jaya, say just once – Uday, if you do not come back, I will marry someone the very next day," he laughed and hugged her.

Jaya would then start sobbing and would put her head on his shoulder, "Uday, why do you say such ominous things."

"Jaya, I'm only teasing you. Your love has engulfed me. I will not be able to live without you. Let's hold on to these lovely moments forever."

"Uday, what will happen to me if you do not come back? God, take me away before that happens," she would continue sobbing.

By October 26, Uday had joined his Unit. After Tawang fell, it was critical to hold on to Se-La Pass. Our Army started to fortify its position. It's not easy to fortify new positions, that too against the dangerous and cunning Chinese. We had nothing as compared to them – no adequate clothing, no proper ammunition, or arms. It's not easy to make fortifications at 14000 feet in the intense cold.

I would shudder thinking of all this.

But all this had been accomplished by our brave *faujis*.

Somewhere in this tough battle, our strategy had crumbled. The enemy had turned out to be treacherous and crafty. Our strategy proved to be no match to the Chinese strategy. Our top Generals and strategists could not make out the head or tail of it, what to speak of our political bigwigs? Nobody had anticipated that the Chinese would actually attack us. We were still patting our backs on our so-called diplomacy of *'Hindi Chini Bhai Bhai'*.

The Chinese had already captured Tawang but our strategists had no clue of their intentions. They had never anticipated that the Chinese would ever capture Tawang. When after the capture of Tawang, the Chinese were lying low, our strategists believed that their assumption was right. Little did they realize that this was the lull before the storm. The Chinese had fortified their positions on the advanced posts within a month. By the time our troops began planning of building bunkers on the treacherous slopes, the Chinese had already build cemented roads and bunkers, so that their advancing troops could be reinforced with all types of help, including arms, ammunition and supplies. Their far sightedness and adequate preparations made them better off. However, we outmatched them in valour.

Shubha and I often wondered about the treacherous Chinese and sometimes asked each other, "What would have Jaya gone through after Uday mama left? She would have felt that there was no future for her." Would she have forgotten the time they had spent together? She would not have forgotten it even now.

Mummy recalls that even afterwards, Jaya would not believe that Uday would never come back. In her utter helplessness, she felt like dying. But love would overcome this helplessness and rekindle hope. She would listen to the news, read every newspaper and visit the families of other Officers. Consoling others would in turn, somehow, console her. Her tears had dried up and her very existence had crumbled, but she still could not accept that Uday would never come back. Mummy had spoken of this many times.

"Neeraja didi, why did Uday not promise me that he would come back? He had just come after the victory in Goa. He had then said with so much conviction, "Jaya, I have come back for you." Where has that conviction gone now? Didi, Uday will come back... won't he?" Perhaps, mummy had no words to console Jaya. She could hardly console herself, how could she have consoled Jaya.

"Didi, Uday loved me so much. How could he leave me and go? When he has to come back, why did he not marry me before going?" Mummy had no answers to this also. I would often think about this and become sad.

Shubha would ask, "Wouldn't Jaya have wanted to leave Lucknow, after all her dreams had been shattered here?"

Even today, if Jaya were to visit Lucknow, wouldn't so many memories come flooding back to her. When she would get down at the Charbagh station, she might perhaps remember: Is this not the same tea-stall? Is this not the old Wheeler's bookshop, and is this not the same waiting room, the same platform where they had met for the last time?

Everything was still very much in place, yet where was he who gave it life and meaning? If she would close her eyes, wouldn't everything appear to be just as before? As if Uday would step out from behind and gently cover her eyes with his hands. She would feel the same familiar touch, the same warm breath on her neck.

God's will, fate, destiny... were mere words that would not have been able to console her.

However hard she would have tried not to let Uday's memories come and haunt her, it would be of no avail. That obstinate guy would break all her resolve to shut out old memories, and he would eagerly come back and hold her once again in his arms.

Whenever she would have walked past the Officer's Mess on Kasturba Road, she would have felt lonely and miserable. The two had often met there; she would be sipping coffee sitting in front of the fireplace and Uday would be looking at her.

"Uday, why do you keep on looking at me like this? Stop that!"

"What happens when I keep on looking at you like this, Jaya?"

"Uday, you will never look at me like this. Promise me."

"I promise you, Jaya, I will always keep on looking at you like this, even when I am no more." Jaya would then look at him in mock anger.

One morning, when she had gone to meet Uday at the Mess, he was having breakfast.

"What will you have, Jaya?"

"I don't want to eat these cornflakes or these idlis and dosas. Get me something nice and spicy."

"What do you mean by spicy?"

"Something like *samosas* or *paani-puri*."

"Jaya, are you in such a hurry to eat those things? Good you told me," he said lovingly.

"Uday, I am going to kill you – *zara Mess se bahar to chalo, phir batati hoon*."

When I thought of those by-gone days, it seemed impossible that so many years had passed. Whenever my sadness brimmed over, I would question myself, "Did all this happen so long ago?"

It certainly doesn't seem so. Mummy and nana speak of it as if it were yesterday. What would have happened in the war? Col Mehta, Major Singh, Capt Sinha, Capt Uday Sharma and Lt Sanjeev Singh were last seen on the intervening night of 18th and 19th November, 1962.

The official version was: "Missing in action."

Where had all of them vanished? Why hadn't any of them come back? So many would be eagerly waiting for them to come back home. What would they have been thinking in their last moments? All of them had been together in those last moments. What would have happened to them? Would there have been anyone around to shed even a tear for them? In that last moment there would not have been even a stray leaf, let alone a flower, that would have fallen on them.

These questions and many others have always saddened me. I have often struggled with the answers to them, but have never given up.

"Only you can find these answers," my heart would tell me.

The passage of time only strengthened my resolve.

3

My first meeting with Dev was a strange albeit beautiful coincidence. It would probably not be correct to call it pure coincidence. Even after so many years, Dev gives credit to destiny.

"Mrinalini, we haven't met just by chance. God Almighty must have had something in His mind for us, otherwise how would someone like you meet an ordinary *fauji* like me?"

"It's strange that someone who wields guns, can speak like this."

I was returning from Nagpur at that time. I had decided to travel at the last moment, so the seat was not confirmed. While going, the train had met with an accident and had reached Nagpur eight hours late. The return ticket, too, was wait-listed. The train was to leave Nagpur in the evening and reach Lucknow the next afternoon. My friend Hussain, who was with the railways, had somehow managed to get my ticket confirmed.

"No one can throw you out of the train in my jurisdiction," Hussain had assured me. He had even confirmed the seat number over the phone.

When I got on the train, the two passengers sitting in front of me looked like they were *faujis*. They had two huge trunks on which their NDA numbers could still be seen inscribed. A similar trunk is still kept with a lot of care in our house. Oh! The amount of luggage these people carry. There are helmets too, which means they must be carrying their bikes as well. Even if they have to go out for a month, they always carry their bikes.

Ahmed Hussain and Mohammed Hussain's soulful, *"Mausam aayenge jayenge"* was playing on their tape recorder. "Dev, this song has become your trademark," I still tease him. But at that time, I was upset that after getting a confirmed seat with such difficulty – my night's sleep would go for a six. These two are bound to drink the night away, and to keep going out many times to smoke,, get down at every station, talk loudly and look at the railway time table every now and then.

One of the Officers said, "Ma'am, don't sit here. This is reserved for some ma'am who is to board at Nagpur. The attendant made us vacate the berth for her from Hyderabad itself."

I kept quiet.

The train started to move. After a while the train superintendent came and enquired if I was comfortable and I thanked him. The two *faujis* ignored this and pretended to read their books.

Though afraid that the two would start to drink at night, I put up a bold front and continued to read my book. When I still could not sleep, I closed my eyes tight and tried hard to sleep again. By then, the two were busy playing cards.

Then, one of them said, "Sir, this is turning out to be a pleasant journey."

"I had looked at the chart carefully at Hyderabad. I knew that a nice co-passenger is going to board at Nagpur," the other replied.

This irritated me. For one, I was not able to sleep, and on top of it, I had to put up with their nonsense.

The train stopped at some station and they got down to get some tea.

On returning, one of them remarked, "What lovely feet," looking at my feet and sipping his tea.

"This face, too, is unforgettable."

The one admiring my feet was Dev.

Dev to this day says, "Mrinalini, you have the loveliest feet I have ever seen. I had fallen in love with them when I saw them for the first time that night on the train. Your feet are lovelier than all the faces I have seen."

It was morning when I woke up. The train had reached Jhansi, and I got down to buy the morning papers. When I returned the two Officers were going to have their tea.

"Ma'am, will you have some tea?" one of them passed me a glass of tea.

We got talking as we sipped tea.

"Where are you going?" I enquired.

"I am Captin Dev Sharma, and this is Major Mohan. We are going to Allahabad. We are returning from Bangalore after completing a course. And what about you?"

"I am Mrinalini Sharma. I am in the IAS, and I am going to Lucknow."

After asking about their Units, when I enquired, "From which course of the NDA are you?" Both of them were astonished. "You seem to know a lot about the Army... any *fauji* connection?" I always laugh at Dev's funny style of speaking English. It had seemed funny initially but now I am used to it. But at that time I had said, "My mama, Capt Uday Sharma was also in the Army. He was from the tenth course of the NDA. We lost him in the China war in the NEFA."

"Was it at Se-La, ma'am?" Dev had asked.

"Yes, he had gone to defend the Se-La Pass. It was thought to be impregnable but in the long run it did not prove to be so," I had become sad.

"Our forces had to fight in extremely adverse conditions. Bitter cold, no ammunitions, no proper winter clothing, depleting strength... but they still fought," Major Mohan spoke slowly.

"I have always wanted to visit mama's Unit and also the Se-La Pass. God only knows when. I have often thought of it," I replied.

"Ma'am, you will definitely go there someday. When you do, remember me as the person who told you that you will definitely make it someday," Dev had said confidently.

While talking to each other, we had exchanged addresses and telephone numbers. They had nice address books but I only had a crumpled Mess bill from Nagpur. They wrote their addresses on it. I still have that torn Mess bill with me, kept safely along with the PCO bill for the first ever phone call that I had made to Dev, those platform tickets when I had gone to see him of at the railway station, parking tickets for the car, entry tickets for the airport, and boarding passes of the flights we took together.

"I had thought that mem saab would have thrown that tattered piece of paper with our addresses and phone numbers into the waste bin the very next day," Dev would later say, laughing.

Manu, my lovely little daughter, had come to receive me at the station. This was the first time I had been away from her for so long. I got down from the train and picking Manu up, started to walked out. Then, suddenly remembering the two Officers, I turned back to say good-bye. But I could not spot them.

Later, Dev told me that Major Mohan had said, "Ma'am has left without even saying good-bye."

"Sir, her daughter had come and picking her up, she left," Dev had replied.

Dev believes, "Mrinalini, because you did not say good-bye that day, we have been destined to meet again and again." He never bids good-bye and always says "see you." Whenever, in anger or to tease him I say "bye", he always asks me to take my words back.

Dev had professed his love to me for the first time in a very special way. His Unit was to move to Kashmir soon, but the date of departure of the advance party had not been decided. He had gone to the Ranges for exercises in February. Very little could be known regarding his whereabouts. It was difficult for him to call from the PCO. The firing practice would last through the nights, and five days had already passed. What do you do when you do not hear at all from someone with whom you are used to speaking practically every day and about whom you think day and night?

After an endless wait the phone finally rang. It was eleven in the night. I was drinking tea and listening to Dev's favourite *gazal, "Mausam aayenge jayenge."* He would always hum or listen to this very *gazal* since we had met.

"Mrinalini, haven't you slept as yet?" It was Dev.

"I was waiting for your call. How are you? When are you coming back? Do you know how many days it has been since we have last spoken?"

"It's exactly 5 days, 16 hrs., 34 mins. and 25 secs., since I have left Allahabad," he laughed.

"What kind of an answer is that?" I had also started laughing.

"Mrinalini, I love you. I love you a lot," saying this he put the phone down.

I was speechless. I could not react. After a while I realised that I had lived that immortal moment which will always be with me. Dev was so sure of his love and of himself that he did not need to wait for an answer from me. I could not have said no, anyway.

4

Dev and I had met by chance but soon realized that our destinies were intertwined. Dev had sent a card for the new year. I had replied to his first card rather formally and that too in the month of March.

'Dear Capt Sharma,' is what I had addressed him, as. Dev's card too had reached me only in February. He teases me to this day, "I had sent you the card so lovingly but you replied with a 'Dear Capt Sharma.'"

Then, by June 1999, the Kargil situation became critical. I thought Capt Sharma's Unit would have moved to the forward area. I wanted to send good wishes to him. It was a tradition in our family to always extend good wishes whenever a *fauji* moved to a forward area on a posting or on exercise, and later when he came back safely, to thank God. Since childhood, I have seen mummy wishing 'good luck', and 'come back safely' to even those she did not know personally. I had barely managed to take some time off in my very busy schedule to buy a 'best wishes' card for Dev. But, it still took a little time, and my boss got pretty cut up about it.

With the war now imminent, Dev and I had come even

closer, and 'Capt Sharma' soon became 'Dear Dev.' I also wrote, "I pray for your long life. Come back safe," on the card.

I would often think of Dev and how would he be. However, many a time I forgot to look out for his reply. Whenever the war was mentioned, Capt Dev Sharma would suddenly come to my mind. At home, mummy was deeply engrossed in all the news about the war. Reading the newspaper, she would lament, "These newspapers only mention so many Officers and so many *jawans* have been martyred. They do not even bother to mention their names. Earlier the name, rank and the place to which they belonged would be mentioned."

Many a time, Shubha would ask her, "Mummy, what is the latest in your Kashmir file?" Mummy would maintain her silence and continue to read the newspapers and listen to the news.

Then, suddenly one day in October, Dev called up. I was not home, so mummy spoke to him. When I got back she said, "Mrinalini, there was a call for you."

"Who was it?" I was surprised.

"Someone known to you," mummy replied, trying to create suspense. "I have been asked not to disclose the name. This person will call again tomorrow night. Try and guess who could it have been."

"Mummy, please tell me who it was?" I asked a bit impatiently.

"Perhaps someone you had met on a train?" she smiled.

I knew at once that it had to be Capt Dev Sharma. He called up late that night and spoke for a long time.

"Please put the phone down. You would have already spent quite a lot on this call by now."

At this, he had laughed and said, "Ma'am, we *faujis* are not fortunate enough to speak to someone like you every day. So let me exhaust my quota of good luck right now."

Now, when that I look back, I realise that the time that would inch by earlier, had now started to fly, after Dev had come into my life.

"Dev came into my life like the coming of spring after a hard winter. Just as the warmth of the sun brings everything back to life, all that was almost dead in the cold of the winter. This love has given me a new life."

When I first met Dev my life was in a disarray. I felt that all my efforts to pick up the broken pieces of my existence and to put them together once again, seemed to have failed. I was engulfed by deep despair. I would pretend to be calm in front of mummy and Manu. But I had become totally hollow from within, so much so that even a touch could shatter me.

Mummy had instilled inner strength in me since childhood, "Mrinalini, I have made you so strong that you will never have to lean on a man's shoulder for anything."

But I would long to lean my head on Dev's shoulder. I had lived through long and dark and difficult days. He had come into my life as a complete stranger and had gradually become a friend and then, one fine day, he had become my very existence. I do not know when and how Dev's love encompassed me totally and completely.

This love gave me a sense of fulfillment and emotional stability. There was a feeling of security that he would always be with me during good times and bad. It felt as though my existence was because of him.

Everyone had noticed this change in me ever since I had met Dev. Shubha was the first to notice it. Mummy had also remarked, "My *bitiya* is now happy once again. Mrinalini dear, we had almost forgotten your tinkling laughter. You always liked to dress up but lately you had stopped doing that. Since your school days you would say, "My passion in life is good clothes, good music, good friends and good books." Without these, life is meaningless for Mrinalini Sharma. This is a welcome change. Our good old days have come back."

However, it was difficult for me to accept this love. There was a continuous tussle between my mind and my heart. My mind would question, "Mrinalini, will the world accept this relationship? Even Dev's family might not accept it easily. Friends and acquaintances may laugh at us. They might say that such relationships do not last. Everyone would have something to say. Would there be no one who would wish happiness for us?"

I would torment myself thinking all this. I would be shattered. It would be almost impossible to put the pieces back together, until Dev's love would call out. Then, I would find myself complete and secure in his heart. This love would once again lead me back to him.

This would take weeks and I would take out the anger and frustration on myself. Many a times I tried to distance myself from Dev. But distance never mattered to Dev. He always felt that we were never separated by distance and were always together.

Sometimes, I would suddenly wake up in the middle of the night. As it is, I would spend sleepless nights. When I would come to terms with the realities of my relationship, the thought of Jaya would invariably come to my mind and sadden me. A big tragedy had ended a lifetime of happiness for her. What if something like this were to happen to us? Were Dev and I destined to be together? I would shudder just thinking about this. But Dev had accepted our love and the ups and downs that came with it.

"Mrinalini, come along with me and surrender to my love. Why this tussle? For once, give your happiness and sorrows to me and let's move on. Every moment after this will be ours and only ours, forever."

When I would still keep quiet he would ask in despair, "Mrinalini, what is it that you really want?" I would still not be able to say anything, but would think, "Dev, hearing all this really consoles me. But I still don't know what to expect from this love of ours?"

A beautiful relationship had developed between Dev and Manu, and now they understood each other very well. I still remember when Dev had come to our house in Lucknow for the first time, Manu had been a child. Dev had affectionately introduced himself extending his hand, "Hello, I am Dev."

"Hello, I am Manu. What do you do?"

"I am in school just like you. Look, what all I have got for you!"

Saying this, he pulled out chocolates and toffees from his pockets. Manu giggled in delight and asked, "How many more pockets do you have? Are there some more chocolates in your pocket?"

Even now Manu says sitting in Dev's lap, "When you had come to our house for the first time, you were wearing a long black coat and you had brought a lot of chocolates and you already looked like a *chocolate ki dukan.*"

Whenever Dev visited us, Manu's happiness knew no bounds. She would jump on to his lap or climb on to his shoulders. When we would go out, she would proudly sit in the front seat next to him and ask, "Why do you live so far away? Why can't you come here more often?"

Whenever Dev called up from Kashmir, Manu would have a list of complaints against me, "Dev, mummy doesn't allow me to watch TV. She has a new Barbie in her cupboard but she is not giving it to me. Why don't you tell her to give it to me, and why don't you come soon. I miss you a lot."

"Mrinalini, why are you unnecessarily trying to discipline her? Let her do what she wants. Will she play with the Barbie once she grows up?"

"Both of you are compelling me to do what I feel is not right," I would say, but Manu would prevail upon me. Sometimes, I got annoyed and would say, "Dev I am her mother and not her enemy."

"Don't bother the child. I shall look into this once I get back, then you can dictate your terms on me. Treat Manu like a child."

Whenever Dev would come on leave, Manu's wish list would be ready in advance. Books, pens, Maggie, chips, toffee, chocolates, Barbie. "Bring everything," she would tell him.

"When you come we will go out for coffee and ice cream every day." Manu would tell him lovingly and looking at me, would say making faces, "This mummy only troubles me, telling me not to do this, not to do that... not to watch TV, sleep early… so we will not take her anywhere with us."

It was difficult for the calls to get through from Kashmir and on top when sometimes Dev would speak for a short while, I would say, "Why are you putting the phone down in such a hurry. Let's talk for some more time."

He would laugh, "Aren't you worried about my phone bills now? I call you so often, just like a husband giving his entire salary to his wife to run the house; I pay this *PCO-waala* my entire salary. It's as if I am married to the telephone department itself!"

Dev lived his life with great integrity. "I believe in and do whatever is true and correct," he would always maintain.

Sometimes, he would get into argument with his seniors, and would often support his juniors. His well wishers would often advise him, "Dev why do you get into trouble with everyone? Your public relations are zero. What will happen in the future? Give up your philosophy of right and wrong and learn to please your seniors."

To this he had a standard reply, "I stick to my philosophy of right and wrong, only for my own satisfaction and not to run down others or to show my superiority. That's why

I exist. This satisfaction gives meaning to my life." May be this conviction of right and wrong was the foundation of our relationship.

"Mrinalini, even if you are not with me forever, at least promise to give me all your sorrows. In turn, I will share all my happiness with you. Trust me, I will keep on loving you, forever."

But was it that easy for me to forget my past hurts, even if I wanted to? Giving all your sorrows to your loved ones and sharing their happiness seemed to be a part and parcel of dreams. The harsh reality of life was different. Whenever I would lean on Dev's shoulder, it would feel as if my problems had lessened. But, very soon, I would start quarreling with him for no rhyme or reason.

Shubha would often advise me, "Mrinalini, why do you always end up fighting with him? If you get after someone, only God can help him."

I had proven this to be true with my frequent quarrels with Dev.

Once Dev had said, "Mrinalini why do you quarrel so much with me? What is it that you want? Are you trying my patience? Dev is a very patient man. Do you still have any doubts? I have already surrendered my heart to you. It's an unconditional surrender. If there is someone in your life before whom there are no pretensions, no formalities and there is hundred per cent commitment, then life becomes so easy. Just for once try loving me like this and see the happiness that it will give you. You have already killed me with your love, then why fight?"

I had been let down in life before. I was afraid to fall in love. So Dev's promise of love scared me. It was true that I loved Dev, was committed to him, but the bitterness of past experiences in life still lingered on. Trust and faith, once lost, are difficult to get back. There was a unknown fear that would haunt me.

If something would happen to Dev… then how will I live? I would be tempted to surrender myself completely to him. This invariably happened when he would be posted in a forward area and there would be no means for me to convey this to him.

I recall Dev saying, "Darling, try falling in love like me." But I would not be able to do that.

I would write innumerable letters to Dev all of which eventually ended up in the paper shredder in my office. Not a single word from these letters ever reached Dev.

"Dev, since I cannot say to you that I love you, listen to my heart," I would say to myself.

But I would end up feeling sad. Our lives continued like this for five years. How long could one live in such uncertainty? Ever since the Unit had moved to Kashmir from Allahabad, forget meeting him, even speaking to him on the phone was difficult. Dev had come on leave many times. In the meantime, he had been promoted to Major. After being promoted, he had called, "Darling, from today my name has changed."

"Is this a joke? You always said that you'll love me forever and if you ever stopped loving me, you will change your name. Has that day come when you will change your name?"

"My name has changed, but for a different reason."

"What is the reason, Dev? Stop troubling me like this," I couldn't take it any more.

"Darling, from today I will be known as Major Dev Sharma," he laughed.

"Oh Dev, congratulations! I am so happy. You scared me to death. Don't pull my leg like this ever again." I was overwhelmed.

After his promotion, Dev had said to Shubha, "What difference does it make whether I am a Major or a Captain. There will be no changes in my life. It will continue to be the same – duty, Mess, bachelor's accommodation and annual leave. Everyone asks me what is the hurry for me to go on leave? I have no issues like most other people do – someone is getting married, someone's wife is pregnant, it's someone's child's first birthday or it's someone's wedding anniversary. And this is true indeed, I have no wife waiting for me to come home for *Teej* or *Karvachauth*. My life has become a question mark. Shubha, I feel so low and disillusioned at times. It is as if I have nothing to look forward to in life."

Hearing this from Shubha, I was flooded with regret. It was partly destiny and partly my own doing that was to be blamed. I was suddenly reminded of my earlier folly. In the beginning I had heard fleeting rumours that Dev was going steady with a girl. I don't know what had been the fate of that relationship. I had never tried to find out. Once, he had philosophically observed, "One never realizes when someone gradually becomes such an important part of one's existence. By the time you become aware of it, life has moved on. It's a strange feeling. There is tranquility, and one is not alone even in solitude. There is only one single thought at all times."

I had tried to console him, "Dev don't be disheartened. Life does not stop if that one special person is not in your life."

I thought Dev had become emotional because of a past relationship. But now, when I think of my stupidity, I am embarrassed. At that time, although Dev had kept quiet, I am sure he must have been exasperated. He would have cursed himself, for he had fallen deeply in love with me, and here I was, so naive about it. Later, he would tease me, "How come you have managed to become such a high ranking officer? I am sure UPSC would have given you some bonus marks for that sweet smile and for your beautiful handwriting."

5

The idea of performing Uday mama's *shraddh* haunted me. How shall I do it? Will the *pandits* at the Holy *sangam* of Allahabad let a woman perform it? I didn't want to ask just any one and every one about this sacred ceremony. How will I tell mummy? How will I broach this subject with her? Should I tell her at all? It was a big dilemma for me. Having pondered over it for a long time, one day, I finally asked her, "Should we perform Uday mama's *shraddh*? They say that the soul does not attain *nirvana* till the *shraddh* is performed." Mummy remained silence. It was so much like her. She has always been a person of a few words. And if it was something important or personal, she takes her own time to open up. Had I even got ten per cent of her patience and composure, my life would have been so much better. After a few days, mummy said, "*Panditji* had come. He said if the exact date of death is not known, then the *shraddh* should be done at the Holy *sangam* on the day of *pitramoksha amavasya.*"

"Should I ring him up?" I asked.

"He had come today. The *shraddh* must be performed in Allahabad. "

I wonder if he will be able to spare the time to come with us? And on that particular day, the *pandits* at the *sangam* don't permit any outsider to perform *puja* at the *sangam*.

I didn't know what to say.

After some time, she said, "I have spoken to kaki in Allahabad. She will arrange for everything. But I don't wish to stay with her."

Kaki was a distant relative. She was eager to assist, and welcomed us when we arrived in Allahabad. Her daughters got all the stuff for the *puja* and made all other arrangements. Kaki only briefed us about the rituals. After all the preparations were done, she accompanied us to the *sangam*.

She told me, "Mrinalini, you are like Uday's daughter. I think, you should perform the rituals." The *Panditji* was a good person, and he understood our feelings. He allowed me to perform the rituals.

We had reached Allahabad a day prior to the ceremony, mummy, Shubha, Manu and I. Dev had also returned to Allahabad that morning. I went to the Officers' Mess to meet him. We were meeting after many months. We had so much to talk about. On one hand I was happy to meet Dev, but on the other, I was pretty emotional thinking about Uday mama. When I reached the Mess, memories came flooding back. As I had always done in the past, I reached Dev's old room, room number 13, by the stairs at the back. The same room number 13 where we had spent countless mornings and evenings.

When Dev was posted here, I used to stand in the balcony, waiting for him to return for lunch, looking at the trees and falling leaves. Once again, everything appeared to be just the same, yet so different. I remember telling him once, "13 is an unlucky number, change your room."

"You have always come to this room. Every time you have gone, you have come back again to this very room. I have re-lived every moment that I have spent with you here. I will never change this room. Please don't ask me to do that ever again."

I still remember those 19 stairs. How many times had I climbed these very stairs with sheer joy. When Dev was leaving for Kashmir, I had gone to see him off and had climbed down these very stairs with a heavy heart.

Emerging back from the memory lane, I rushed to Dev's room. The door was not latched, but I waited outside. Hearing my footsteps, Dev came out laughing and said, "Hi, how are you mem'saab?"

I quietly sat down in the chair. "You wanted me to come, and here I am at your service ma'am. But why the long face? Do you know, your left cheek hangs a bit more than your right one? I can sense your left cheek hanging even when you talk to me on phone," he said, trying to amuse me.

By then, tears were rolling down my cheeks. Dev came from behind and put his hands around my shoulders. I turned and hugged him. I couldn't say anything and continued crying.

That day was the first time I spoke to Dev about Ajit. By now, I had surrendered myself, my past, my present and my future to Dev because he loved me so much.

"Dev, Ajit and I were married. He was a strange man, very practical, bordering on the selfish, He lived only for himself, and was not bothered at all about others. Some people derive all happiness through their own achievements. Ajit was one of those. We met, and within two months he proposed to me. Without thinking at all, I said 'yes'. I did feel strange, realising that I had said 'yes' in a hurry to the most important decision of my life. Later, I told Ajit, "We should not hurry. Let's give it some more time." He was shrewd. He showed a lot of understanding then, and said, "my decision will remain the same, the rest is up to you." Had he tried to blackmail me emotionally or had quarreled with me over this, the story would have been over then and there. But he knew me well. By not making an issue and patiently hearing my point, he made me feel guilty. Eventually, his cunning paid off."

"After few days of dilemma, I agreed to marry him." Staring at the blank wall and feeling absolutely hollow, I was narrating the most unpleasant days of my life to Dev. "Mrinalini, I don't want to know anything about your past. I have asked you to give me all your sorrows. So, just give those to me. Don't share, but give them to me completely," he said.

But I went on. Today I wanted to tell Dev everything about my past. Ajit used to feel that there is no bigger fool than Mrinalini Sharma. In fact, he wanted to get all his work done through me. I was never a practical person. I have always been honest and forthright. I never knew how to misuse my position for selfish goals. There was no difference between Mrinalini, the teacher, or Mrinalini, the officer. I never felt that it was below my dignity to go to office in a rickshaw or to travel in sleeper class. But Ajit, … Dev didn't want to hear anything more, "Stop, Mrinalini."

"No Dev, let me speak. I don't want to hide anything from you. I am not ashamed of speaking about my past. Actually, I would not have been able to withhold myself even if I wanted to. Ajit would often cajole me to use my influence, my power, and my position. And when I refused, he would get upset. He would frequently lose his temper and snap at me. Things began to turn ugly between us. I soon realized that I had made a big mistake. But now that I had realised my mistake, what next?"

"Finally, Shubha and mummy saved me from this unpleasant situation. You know, Dev, I had married against the wishes of my family. Mothers are always large-hearted. Mummy bailed me out. Since childhood, I had shared my woes, my problems, my troubles and my sorrows only with my mother. She always found a solution for me. Finally, I took charge of my life. Mummy started taking care of Manu, and my life returned to normal."

Ajit tried hard to win me back. Shubha made sure that my resolve did not weaken, and soon Ajit and I parted ways. It was good that Manu was too small to understand or be effected by any of this.

I was sobbing uncontrollably by now. Dev listened patiently, with his arms around me. The past, which had always scared me, flashed past my eyes. Though I was detached now, I could still feel the pain. Dev couldn't have expressed in words what his loving touch was able to convey at that time. I still have no words to describe that feeling.

"Dev, I continued to blame myself for a long time. Trying to find my fault. I wish those three dreadful years had have never come in my life. Better times slowly returned. My anger and self pity slowly ebbed. Outwardly, I maintained that everything was fine, but mummy could always see my pain. I would tell her, "Mummy, I have forgotten the past, just like a bad dream." But how I wish I could tear off those three years from the book of my life. Although now, I have at least thrown them in the waste paper bin." Having said all this, I felt much better.

Only I knew what I had endured when this storm was surrounding me. But I never let anyone know of it. Leave aside the inner turmoil, no one even saw the tremors outwardly. I don't know how mummy could always read my mind. We never said anything to each other, but always managed to read each other's thoughts.

I composed myself and said, "Dev, I have forgotten my bitter past. Earlier, I would wonder "Why did this happen to me" But now, I only wish that we should have met earlier. You have come into my life, and now I have no regrets whatsoever."

"Mrinalini, why do you get perturbed by these small things? Have faith in me. I have always loved you and my love for you will only grow. Why rue over the past, a past that you have thrown out of your life? Why feel sad about it? Why talk about it? If you do want to treasure anything, then let it be our love." He said lovingly, taking me into his arms.

The *shraddh* ceremony was to be performed the next day. On reaching the *sangam*, I sat on the banks of the holy Ganga, along with Shubha, Mummy and Manu.

The *pandit* started the rituals. "Close your eyes, join your hands and remember your mama whose *shraddh* is being performed," he said.

Uday mama's photo from when he was commissioned instantly came to my mind. His smiling face, straight out of the photograph, floated right in front of my eyes. I had not seen him in my life, but his image was crystal clear in my mind.

The rituals began. I made a *pinda* for the *pinda daan*, covered it with a cloth and offered it *til* and water as *tarpan*. We then took a boat to the *sangam* to immerse the *pinda* in the holy waters. Before offering the *pinda* in the *sangam*, I prayed, "Uday mama, wherever you are and in whatever form you are in, may God give you peace. Whatever good you have done in your life, let that be with you forever. May God grant your *mukti*. Let there be no earthly attachments constraining you."

Thereafter, I immersed the offerings into the holy waters of the *sangam*.

While returning, I thought of Jaya. Ever since I had come to Allahabad, thoughts of Jaya had kept haunting me. In my mind, nothing could separate Uday and Jaya. I visualized them to be together always and never apart. But destiny had thrown them apart. Perhaps there still existed an unseen bond between them. Actually, I felt they had never been apart. Why were they destined to go through all this? Jaya had everything except Uday. The tide of time had swept away their happiness. Who could have had an answer to this except God? I didn't notice tears that had started rolling down my cheeks.

We have not been able to accept the passing of Uday mama. Fate or God's will, nothing has offered any solace. I had never seen Jaya. But since childhood, whenever I think of her, the photograph taken on their engagement would come to my mind. Young and pretty, Jaya, barely out of her teens, was wrapped in a sari. Almost blushing while slipping the engagement ring onto Uday mama's finger. And Uday mama glancing at her lovingly. I am sure she remembers that loving glance even today.

Dear God... why did you separate them so ruthlessly? Wiping away my tears, I moved towards the car, leaving some money for the boatman.

After the *shraddh* we went to an orphanage to feed the children there.

While returning from the *sangam*, I offered prayers at the famous Hanuman temple and then went to meet Dev. I felt absolutely hollow and empty as if all the silence and loneliness had engulfed me.

Even after one departs from this world, there must be something which is definitely left behind, something which seeks *nirvana*. Uday mama was so much in love with Jaya when he had departed from this world... would he be looking for salvation from love? Will this *shraddh* ultimately free him from all worldly ties? Will he be able to free himself from this unfulfilled love? Probably not. For that, he would have to come into this world, and relive his love for Jaya. Even after so many years, Uday mama was tied to Jaya... or was it she who was tied to him? Anyway, after this *shraddh*, even if he has not got salvation, his soul definitely will not wander. When I reached the Officers' Mess, Dev was listening to music.

Seeing me in a somber mood, he came to me and took me in his arms. Holding back my tears, I gave him *prasad* from the Hanuman temple. He quietly took a piece and said, "Your belief is very firm, Mrinalini. You've wanted to perform the *shraddh* for such a long time and now that you have done it, how are you feeling? I wanted to come but...."

"Dev, why didn't you come? You should have. You had every reason to be there. Are we separate from each other? I am like your shadow. How can I be away from you? I am always with you." I said lovingly.

"When there is no sun, there are no shadows," he said in a serious tone.

"After the sun sets, this shadow becomes one with you. It exists because of you, around you and is with you at all times. Look at this," showing him the knot on my *dupatta*, I said, "You always ask, why I tie this knot? Whenever you are not with me when you should have been, I tie this knot. It symbolises that you are always with me. You were very much with me even today. How could you not have been with me, when I was fulfilling my wish?" I leaned on his shoulders as he caressed my hair.

6

After Uday mama's *shraddh*, I was keen to meet Jaya's parents. After a lot of effort, I was able locate Col Mishra's residence on Faizabad road. Mummy had told me long back, "It's a big house that could be seen from the road." Now, there were lots of shops in the open space in front of the house. There was a name plate on the gate – Col A.K. Mishra. Though time had not left any visible impression on it, but a lot had changed since. I entered through the gate and came to the main door. I was feeling a bit odd. There was a strange hesitation in my mind. I felt like turning back, but composed myself and knocked on the door. It felt as if I was knocking on the door of the past.

After some time, an elderly man appeared at the door. Seeing a total stranger, he seemed to be perplexed. Perhaps, many people did not knock on this door very often.

"Yes? What can I do for you?"

"I am Mrinalini Sharma, Neeraja Sharma's daughter. These days I am posted here in Lucknow."

He stared for a while and exclaimed, "Oh! You are Neeraja's daughter, do come in, dear." Holding my hand he led me to the drawing room. He was speaking, more to himself, "After so many years! What a pleasant surprise. Time has really flown and how everything has changed."

He called out to his wife, "Reema, look, who is here." Then added, "It's Mrinalini, Neeraja's daughter."

Mrs Mishra walked in. Even in this age, she looked beautiful. I had heard a lot about her beauty since childhood. She had on a light blue sari. Her hair was neatly tied in a bun. A very pale pink lipstick adorned her lips.

She hugged me lovingly. Sitting next to me, she held my hands and asked, "How is Neeraja? And your sister?

"Mummy is fine. Shubha is in Delhi. She teaches in a college."

After some time, Col Mishra said, "We came to know of the unfortunate news about your father. It was very sad indeed, very untimely. We had gone to meet Neeraja. She had refused to come and stay with her father. That was very brave of her."

Mrs Mishra then asked, "Has Shubha got married? And what about you?"

"Shubha is still single. She hasn't married. My daughter is five and half years old. But now I am single too. My brief marriage ended years ago."

Actually, now I answer this frequently asked question with ease. I have repeated the same answer so many times in my office, to the relatives and at parties. Initially this question always used to put me off balance. I used to get disturbed. At times I used to just keep quiet out of embarrassment. Many a times, I would become irritated, losing my cool. But with time it has changed. May be Dev's love has given me the strength and now I can face the truth easily.

I often think, Manu is mine. She is most precious to me. Whatever else has happened should not bother me. Now, I don't feel as if all that has happened to me. It seems as if it had happened to some other Mrinalini.

Meanwhile, tea was served and we started talking about old times. I asked, "You knew Uday mama since he was a child. I want to know more about him. Please tell me something about him." Mrs Mishra started off, "Uday was a very nice person. Even after so many years, it doesn't appear as if he is not here amongst us. We have spent such happy times in this very drawing room. Whenever he came, he would sit in that particular corner. That place was earmarked for him. None of us have ever been able to sit there. Even if some guest sits there unknowingly, I always make them shift on some pretext."

I thought, why only the chair, probably so many other things in this house must still be missing Uday mama.

Col Mishra could sense the heaviness in the atmosphere and said, "Uday was a very emotional, quiet and loving young man. We would eagerly wait for him to come home on vacation. He would come during his school days in RIMC, and then during his term breaks at the NDA and the IMA. He used to come to us first and then go home."

Mrs Mishra had drifted into the past by now. As if in a trance, she continued, "Uday never got annoyed. Jaya was rather short-tempered and used to quarrel with him frequently for rather silly reasons. If Uday's letters got delayed she would declare, "Never again will I write to Uday." If the train ever arrived late, she would complain, "Uday! My life will be wasted waiting for you at the railway platform... we should build a room here. But Uday would never mind, and always used to laugh it off."

Col Mishra had become pretty emotional by then and said, "When Uday was promoted to Captain, your grandfather, Umakant, and I announced Jaya and Uday's engagement. It was a grand occasion. You must have seen those photos."

Mrs Mishra continued, "That day Jaya had worn a sari for the first time, a light green sari, with a bright yellow border. Neeraja had got her that sari. Jaya was looking pretty. After getting ready she had asked Uday, "And the bangles? And who will help me put them on?" Uday had taken her to the *churiwaala*. She had put on a whole lot of green bangles on both her hands."

Col Mishra was lost in the memories. He said, "When their marriage was fixed and Uday was about to come, I had asked Jaya to stop quarreling with Uday. He was coming from Goa. I said to her, 'There will be other officers of his Unit with him. You are coming along to pick him up. Please be quiet and don't start your complaints right there at the station.' She stayed absolutely quiet. I felt good that my daughter was behaving in a very mature way. Seeing her so quiet, Uday had asked, 'Jaya! Are you alright? I have been narrating grand stories of your fighting skills to everyone in my Unit.' One day, I even told my Commanding Officer, 'Sir, some people are born fighters. It is our bad luck that they are not in the Army.'"

"And that was it." Col Mishra continued, "Jaya's patience gave in. She started her nit-picking then and there." Uday laughed. "That's what I was wondering about. Is Jaya on some kind of a fast today? Otherwise, without quarrelling with me how can she survive?"

"Please tell me something about the war." I requested Col Mishra.

"There was an atmosphere of great uncertainity," he said on a serious note. "Right from Army Headquarters to the NEFA, the entire country was in a turmoil. Nobody knew what the Chinese were upto. Nothing was known with certainty about their intentions, their plans, strengths or position." After a pause, he continued, "Our Army advanced, but we were not at all prepared for war. When Uday's *paltan* reached Se-La, there was nothing there. They had to start from scratch. Se-La Pass was very important. Tawang had already fallen to the Chinese. Now, if Chinese advance was to be halted, Se-La Pass had to be defended at all costs.

I asked him, "Will you please tell me what happened on that fateful day?" I had always wanted to know since my childhood, but was never able to muster the courage to ask nana or mummy.

He was absolutely serious by then and said, "Let me give it a try. You probably will not understand the technical terms and Army lingo... but let me give it a try. The moment Uday's Unit reached Se-La, they were ordered to take defenses in front of the advancing Chinese. They were launched into battle straight away, having been sent from the foothills in Himachal to the treacherous snow covered heights of the Himalayas at 14000 feet."

He got a paper and pen and drew a map. He started to explain. "Two companies of their *paltan* were deployed ahead. The Battalion Headquarters and the Third Company were near Se-La and the Fourth Company was about ten kilometer away on snow-capped peaks. Our Army was preparing to defend Se-La at all costs. Our patrols would go and gather information every day. Our seniors used to think that the Chinese would not attack. There would only be minor scuffles."

He further added, "But in reality, the Chinese were planning to attack with full preparations at the right place and the right time. Our intelligence had failed completely. Col Mehta was Uday's Commanding Officer. After about twenty days had passed like this, on 16th November, when he went for a recce of the forward areas, Uday accompanied him. The patrolling party which had gone ahead informed him about the large scale activities of the Chinese. He himself went ahead and observed a large convoy of the Chinese coming from Tawang. The intentions of the Chinese were becoming clear now. They had constructed a road ahead of Tawang and cleared their supply and maintenance line. They were in a position to attack anytime now. The neighbouring Unit also observed similar large-scale movements of the Chinese.

"When this information was passed to the Brigade Headquarters, they were caught off-guard. The Companies deployed ahead were ordered to fall back to Se-La. But it was not easy to do that as the troops were surrounded by the enemy from all sides. But it had to happen. When the troops started withdrawing, they had to face bullets from all sides. It was difficult to move even an inch. Nobody was able reach back to reinforce Se-La. Some got killed, some lost their way and some, wandering in the jungles, strayed into Bhutan.

"Now Se-La, which was to be defended by the entire Battalion, barely had the strength of a Company, that is, just one-fourth of the required strength. Col Mehta and Uday were there. Lieutenant Singh and a few other soldiers managed to join them after withdrawing amidst heavy enemy fire. They had successfully accomplished the mission of withdrawing and joining the Battalion Headquarters in order to give a bigger fight. All of them were very happy, completely oblivious of the storm that was about to engulf Se-La. The neighbouring Unit was ordered to withdraw, but Col Mehta knew nothing about it. It was probably lack of coordination on part of the Headquarters.

"The vacated positions became ready-made launch pads for the Chinese attack. They attacked Se-La in full strength. A very well prepared defence can withstand one or two attacks of the enemy. The defences at Se-La could not be termed even 'ready', leave aside calling it 'adequate' or 'very well-prepared'. But they fought like tigers."

Col Mishra took a pause, then began to speak again, "The Chinese first attacked in the early hours of 18th November. Against a 100 of our men, they were 5000. Our soldiers still gave them a tough fight and chased them off. But they soon returned. They were a determined lot. They suffered heavy casualties and had to retreat every time they came, but they would regroup and would quickly mount another attack. That was their technique. Generally, a soldier sitting in defence can take on two or three attackers, may be, four at a time. But the Chinese were like *Mahishasur.* If two of them were killed, four more would return. There was no shortage of men in China, anyway. The Chinese Army was the largest Army in the world. They believed in overwhelming numerical superiority. To fight one soldier of ours, they were capable of sending 50-60 of theirs, forget 5 or 6. And they actually did that."

By now, Col Mishra was almost choking with emotion. He paused for a while, took a sip of water and continued, "On 18th November, not once or twice, the Chinese attacked eight times, but were made to retreat every time. Unfortunately, no reinforcement could be sent to our men at Se-La. The Chinese had surrounded them from all sides. Eventually, only few of our men were left, all of them badly injured.The ammunition was about to finish. Another assault – which proved to be the final one – was launched by the Chinese in the night, and this time from three sides. But our bravehearts had sworn to live and die together. A true soldier chooses to die than run away from the battle field. Chanting their battle cry, *Bole So Nihaal, Sat Sri Akaal,* Col Mehta and his brave men, now completely outnumbered, without any ammunition left with them, and badly injured, fought their final battle. After a fierce battle, Se-La eventually fell."

Tears rolling down her cheeks, Mrs Mishra said, "Mrinalini, that was one of the most unlucky days for our country. The Chinese outnumbered us in every way. But our soldiers fought like tigers till their very last breath. They attained martyrdom defending our nation."

I was filled with pride and sorrow at the same time. By now, all of us had become emotional. The atmosphere had become heavy.

Col Mishra continued, "It would have been a long night for those 50-60 men. It was to prove the last night of their lives. God only knows what they would have been thinking. May be, they would have remembered things from their past or may be nothing at all. Now all that is left is memories... memories of Col Mehta and his valiant men."

"When mama didn't come back…," I said, but could not speak anymore. I did not know how to bring up the subject of Jaya. Mrs Mishra guessed my dilemma. She said, "Nothing could have brought more grief and sorrow for us. Jaya was completely shattered. She used to keep awake the whole night, pacing up and down in the verandah or in the garden. Often, she would say to me, "Mummy, nothing will happen to Uday. God can't be so cruel." I would try to console her. She would say "Mummy, when Uday comes back, he'll think all of us are sleeping peacefully, and that no one cares about him. That's why I am keeping awake and waiting for him."

At times, she would doze off, but even at the slightest noise, she would ask, "Uday, is that you? Have you come back at last?" She would often sit under that tree and keep staring at the gate. The winter passed and autumn came, but she would still sit in the garden and keep waiting," Col Mishra said with tears in his eyes.

"I know. Mummy has told me that Jaya went to meet her one day. Her blank eyes clearly told the story of those unfortunate, sad days." She had said to mummy, "Didi, so many days have passed. This calendar has only given me meaningless dates." I couldn't say anything more.

Col Mishra said, "We married off Jaya within a year. I told Rajiv and his father everything. Anyway, I couldn't have hidden it from them. Rajiv is a good man. He really took care of Jaya. He brought her back to reality once again. Jaya also managed to compose herself. Rajiv has retired as a Colonel and they live in Pune now. They have two sons, both of whom have settled abroad."

Mrs Mishra brought out a photo album, and a lot of loose photos of Uday and Jaya. "I am seeing these pictures after years, They were kept aside in an envelope. How happy they look! Seeing these photos one would never imagine what God had in store for them. On the day of her wedding, Jaya locked herself in her room with these photographs. She sat there alone for quite some time. When she came out, she was a changed person altogether. Calmly, she said, "Mummy, please keep these photographs safely with you. I tried to destroy them, but couldn't. Even if I did destroy them, I won't be able to erase Uday's memories and the time that I have spent with him. So far in my life of 19 years, Uday has always been with me, every moment of it. If I take him out of my life, nothing will be left of me. I shall abide by what Daddy has decided, but Uday was there in my life and will always continue to be. No one can ever take his place."

"Can I meet Jaya if I go to Pune?" I asked Mrs Mishra. I had never seen Uday mama, but had always wanted to meet Jaya. I have asked myself, "Were they star-crossed lovers? Was their love destined to end like this? Has time been able to obliterate it? Their love is still emitting the beautiful colours of a rainbow. True love, really, is eternal."

"Why not? You must meet Jaya. She will be very happy that someone from Uday's family has come to meet her." Mrs Mishra said.

"Which Unit is Col Rajiv Kumar from?" I asked.

When Col Mishra mentioned the Unit, I was pleasantly surprised. He was from the same Unit as Dev. I took leave of Col and Mrs Mishra. I couldn't bring myself to tell them that I had performed Uday mama's *shraddh*. I thought it better to let Uday stay alive in their memories.

I had not been a witness to Uday and Jaya's love. But I had heard about it in bits and pieces. I can always put them together for a beautiful picture to emerge. As I grew up, this picture became much clearer and more defined. I had heard so much from mummy and had understood so much without having actually seen any of it.

I was happy because I had just re-lived a past relationship. I was sad because of the tragic and unhappy end of Jaya and Uday's love. It was a strange emotion, very difficult to comprehend.

7

Finally, the day when Dev was to go to Kashmir had arrived. It was towards the end of December in 2000. He had rung me up from the New Delhi railway station. "Mrinalini, I am going. I shall be back the moment I get leave. And please don't hang your face. Bid me a happy farewell. Okay then ... see you, darling."

With a very heavy heart, I thought now it's going to be a long wait for me again. Dev does not have a phone. Connectivity is very poor in the valley. It is very difficult to get through to someone in a remote corner of the valley. And someone who is not very fond of writing letters. But I shall have to keep writing letters. Dev always used to say, "When I get a bunch of your letters, I can't tell you how happy I am. Life becomes more beautiful. I see rainbows everywhere, even inside my bunker. These rainbows need neither rain nor sky. With these rainbows around, even in this loneliness of my post, I keep thinking of you and weaving dreams about you."

I used to laugh and ask, "How can you see rainbows with the Pakistani posts right in front?"

"Mrinalini, you are always with me even in this small bunker. Though ladies are not allowed at posts, you are always with me." Filled with love, Dev continued, "When I receive the parcels that you send, the Adjutant comes to know even without looking at the address that they are meant for me. So many letters come for me and I also get the maximum phone calls from the *mem saab*."

In those days, there were PCOs in the Army exchanges and some civil calls from close relatives would be transferred on Army lines to the personnel posted on forward posts. By now, Dev Sharma had become famous in all the Army exchanges around Baramulla and Uri.

Once, an exchange operator had, by mistake, put my call through to some other Major Sharma from a different Regiment. The weather had been bad, so phone lines were disturbed. The call could be connected only after a lot of effort. The voice from the other end was not very clear. I asked, almost angrily, "Dev, can you hear me? I shall come there and kill you right." The poor 'other' Major Sharma could not understand who this lady was and why was she shouting at him? After composing himself, he very politely replied, "Ma'am, I think you want to talk to Major Dev Sharma. Let me get the call transferred."

Later, this officer met Dev in Baramulla and told him with a sheepish smile "Sir, the other day your call got connected to me by mistake. Ma'am appeared to be angry!"

"Oh, that's her way of showing affection that only I can understand." Dev had said with a hearty laugh.

As a welfare measure, some satellite phones were made available to the Army Units deployed in the forward areas.

These used to be sent from one post to the other. Generally, once a month, when the Sat-phone was available to him, Dev would call. The clarity would be pretty good and we would talk for quite some time. He had watched the movie "Nine Months" then. Talking about it, he said, "Nice kids in the movie. How many do you want, mem saab?"

It was a full-moon night and I was sitting outside on the terrace. I blushed.

"This moon has not set yet. Mrinalini, come here to be with me. I can't bear this separation any longer. When will this long wait be over? Will the seasons just go by? Will I only continue to keep thinking of you, sitting alone here? Will you not come with the seasons? How unlucky I am. This moon can see you, but I can't. Let's watch the moon together from afar."

"Dev, if you are calling me with love, I might just land up there. So be careful. Do you remember you had called me once with such longing and I had come to you?"

I was referring to something that happened about two years ago. Dev was returning from an exercise. He had called up enroute and said, "Mrinalini, I am missing you a lot, can you come now."

"Yes, of course, darling. I am planning to come next week with Shubha." I responded spontaneously.

"What if I am not there then?" Dev said jokingly. "Who knows what may happen tomorrow!" he quipped.

I sensed a strange restlessness in him. I got up, packed some clothes and boarded the first available train to Allahabad.

We kept chatting that whole night, sitting on the stairs of the Officers Mess. God only knows what all we talked about.

"Mrinalini, so much is happening in my life. It has become so beautiful now. I believe in destiny. Now that you love me so much, I am sure the future belongs to us."

I became sad, "Dev, how many justifications will you give? This age difference between us, my past, and..."

"Mrinalini, whether life is easy or hard, depends largely on your life-partner. Please stop denying this love. Are we only destined to meet like this once in a while? Do I not deserve your complete love? The final countdown has begun and the Unit will be moving to Kashmir very soon," he had said with a heavy heart.

"Your being away makes all the difference to me, Dev. How can we overcome the pain of these separations? See how gloomy the night has become now that you are talking of going."

Dev had come to see me off at the station. He hugged me and said playfully, "I need an excuse to take you in my arms, be it to welcome you or to see you off!"

Before Dev's Regiment moved to Kashmir, Shubha and I went to Allahabad again. We reached late in the night. The Mess was closed. Dev had got the dinner to his room. Seeing the amount of food laid out, I joked, "Dev what were you thinking? We cannot eat such a lot. What a waste." I counted the *chapatis*. "18! Wow! Shubha and I can eat at the most two each. Are you going to polish off the rest?" I laughed.

"I am a rustic at heart. People eat a lot in villages. You

better practice making *chapatis*. Otherwise, you only know how to cook rice." he said light-heartedly.

After dinner, we talked late in to the night.

"When I look back, everything appears to be a dream, a beautiful dream. Look how this wonderful time has come and gone by so swiftly. And now, the time has come for me to go so far away," Dev said, looking at me.

"Dev, sometimes it does happen that before we realize, someone comes very close to us and becomes a part of our very existence. We realize it only when he has gone away." Shubha said, and excused herself.

"I have often kept awake at night just thinking of you. My life seems as if I am destined for endless wanderings," I said sadly.

"What 'wanderings' are you talking of Mrinalini? I feel as if I can touch the sky," Dev said, taking my hand into his. We barely noticed that it was already morning.

Whenever I am in Allahabad, I always visit the *sangam* and the Hanuman *mandir*.

When Dev's Regiment was in Allahabad, and even after they had moved out, I continued with my visits to the *sangam* and the temple. Behind the Hanuman temple near the *sangam*, there is a sacred *peepal* tree. I always lit *diyas* under it. When we were going to the temple for the first time, Dev had said, "I shall wait here in the Mess. You go to the temple please."

But Shubha had insisted that he accompany us. Finally, she said to him, "If you don't come along, we shall not go either. We shall return without going to the temple, although I am very keen to go." Dev had accompanied us very reluctantly. Shubha often says to him, "Dev, we had to literally push you to the temple."

In the temple, I asked Dev, "Give me some money. I have to buy stuff for *pooja*." He handed over his wallet without a word. I felt so good to spend money from his wallet. I bought a big *tulsi* garland and *laddoos* for offering at the temple. It was a Saturday, so the temple was crowded. Shubha walked ahead and Dev, very slowly, followed me. We gave the sweets and garlands to the *pujari*. After offering these to Hanumanji, he gave back the sweets and two garlands to us. He also gave Dev a flower, which Dev in turn handed over to me. I tied it to my *duppatta*. Dev looked at me with amazement. We came out of the temple. "Look, everyone is lighting *diyas* under the *peepal* tree. Let's also light some," Shubha said. It was a bit windy, so when I tried to light the *diyas,* the matchstick would blow off. "Give it to me, I will light it for you," Dev said. He managed to light the *diyas* with just one matchstick. It was a wonderful sight – so many *diyas* flickering in the night.

Dev asked, "What have you tied to your *pallu*? I only smiled. I put the garland around Dev's neck. I still do that... everytime we visit a temple together, I put the garland that I get back from the *puja* around his neck.

We moved towards the *sangam*. There was a bit of a chill in the air, but it was pleasant. There, too, people were lighting *diyas* and floating them into the holy Ganga.

"Dev, let us light *diyas*, too." I said to him, taking his hand in mine. It was serene all around us. With Dev beside me, I could hear everything that was unsaid. His mere touch conveyed everything. As they say, the sound of silence is like a sweet melody.

Shubha was walking slightly ahead of us. Dev was walking with his arms around me. After some time, Shubha sat on the banks of the Ganga, looking at the holy waters, deep in thought. She looked absolutely calm and serene. Dev lit some *diyas* and called Shubha to join us. We floated the *diyas* in the *sangam*. The gentle flow of the river took the *diyas* along with it. They floated slowly away from us. I leaned on Dev's shoulders, looking at the *diyas*.

"Let's go back," Dev said. On our way back we were all very quiet. The serenity of the *sangam* still showed on Shubha's face. She appeared to be meditating. She broke the silence after some time, "How peaceful it is over here. This silence and serenity is so beautiful. I felt as if it has seeped right into my soul," she said calmly.

"I told you to ask God for blessings. What did you ask for?" I nudged Dev.

"How could I disobey you? Yes, I did," Dev replied.

"But what exactly did you ask for?" I coaxed him.

"I can ask God for anything. But the one who has to bestow something special does not seem to understand what I have been desiring for so long. She is totally oblivious of my love," he almost whispered.

We had reached his room. I hung the garlands from the temple on either side of the dressing table.

Seeing our reflection in the mirror with garlands around us, he said, "I wish time stops here."

After sometime, Dev called for a drink. I noticed that he was drinking a bit faster today. When it was late in the night, Shubha said, "Let's have dinner."

"Mrinalini, why are you frowning? It's not poison that I am drinking ... though I can drink real poison for you!" he teased me. Before he could realize, I picked up his glass and drank the liquor in it in one gulp. It tasted quite bitter. "Dev, I don't think poison can be worse than this," I spluttered.

By then, dinner was served. I took some food and started eating. Dev made himself another drink, and smiling, said, "Shubha, someone is very angry today. I am going to have to put in a lot of effort to make up with her."

Shubha laughed. I kept my plate aside and without saying anything went to the balcony. Dev followed and stood behind me. I snatched the glass from his hand and threw it down from the balcony. He went inside and brought back all glasses he had and said, "Darling, please break these as well, if they help subside your anger. These glasses are, in fact, lucky to be broken by you."

I kept throwing down glass after glass and he kept handing one glass after the other to me. When none were left, he said, "Are you still angry? There aren't any more glasses left. But otherwise, I am at your majesty's service."

By then I had calmed down, and regretted my brash behaviour. What I had done? "Dev, you are going away. It's hard for me to maintain my composure. We could have talked of something nice. But all you were interested in was your drink," I said, slowly.

"I am sorry, Mrinalini." Dev took me in his arms.

I leaned on his shoulder and asked, "Why do you drink so much? What do you get out of it?"

"I am not addicted to drinking, darling. I get intoxicated the moment you look at me," he said cheerfully.

"How shall I live without you? Look what have you done to me? How will these four months pass without you? Please come back the moment you get leave." I was almost sobbing, "Please... don't go."

"Why do you love me so much? Who can be a bigger extremist than you, in love? There is no beginning or end to your love. Your love is like a flash-flood in the river. It sweeps away everything with it. Try as hard as you can, but you cannot help but get washed away instantly. But I am always scared, what if this river of love were to dry up some day? Mrinalini, please don't let this river of love ever dry up. Let me keep flowing in it forever. I shall never ask where you take me. Even if there is no destination, I can keep flowing in it till eternity."

We continued to talk the whole night. In the morning Shubha and I returned, and the same night Dev too left for Kashmir. He took along the flowers that I had kept in his room. After almost a month, I got this letter from him:

Dear Mrinalini,

I am sure you are fine. I keep thinking of you all the time. There is so much to remember of the beautiful past, but thinking of the future, I get scared at times that can these dark nights get even darker? I always console myself thinking that after these dark nights, a pleasant morning definitely awaits us.

Do you remember our trip to Saugor? It was spring and red *palash* was blooming all around. The entire jungle had become a sea of red. The road through the middle of the thick forest was more like a flower bedecked pathway. You were ecstatic to see those beautiful red flowers. "How beautiful!" you had said. "No other flower can be more beautiful than a blooming *palash*. Why don't people decorate their houses with it? Look Dev, although it stands alone here in this lonely forest, it is spreading happiness and colour all around. What different hues – red, scarlet, crimson, orange and each one more beautiful than the other."

Mrinalini, I am missing you a lot today. I am remembering those *palash* trees. Does the *palash* have only one hue? I always feel it gets all its hues from you. When you are happy and cheerful, it blooms in a pleasant red. When you glance at me with love, it takes on even a brighter shade of red. If, even for a moment you are sad, I don't see any colour in it. I don't even notice that there are flowers all around. It feels as if all the solitude of the jungle has seeped into me. When you lean on my shoulder with love, this jungle of crimson engulfs me like a fire lighting the flame of love within me. They say that Kashmir is heaven on earth. But I have always been stuck by the lack of something here. In this heaven, there is no *palash*. But, whenever I think of you; thousands of *palash* bloom all around me even in this snow, literally thousands and thousands of them all around me in their myriad hues and shades. But I know all these hues are because of you, *jaane kitne rang palash ke, par har rang tumhi se hai.*

Yours

Dev

I sat down to reply, with emptiness within me. I could pen only a few lines:

Ek adhoori lakir guzar jaati hai,

Meri hatheli se tumhari hatheli tak.

Jab dekho isse

Tumhari hatheli se milakar apni hatheli ko,

To lagta hai yeh puri ho gayi.

Alag-alag apni-apni hatheli ko liye,

Hum kab tak yun hi jiyenge adhoori lakir ko liye,

Mitane se mitati bhi nahin...

Jodne se judti hai

Par bas pal bhar ke liye.

8

When Dev came on leave next, we decided to go to Pune. By now I was very keen to meet Jaya. It was time to visit the National Defence Academy. Those past days, to which I had not been a witness, and now when I was returning back to those bygone times, Dev was with me.

Whenever I had re-lived those days, Dev had always been with me. That is why I wanted to go to the NDA with him. Was I, somewhere, trying to meet Uday mama on the pretext of meeting Jaya? Mummy and nana had traversed this same route from Pune to Khadakwasla years ago for Uday mama's Passing Out Parade. Now, years later, Dev and I were traversing the same path all over again. It was difficult to fathom how I felt. Can life change as effortlessly as turning over while asleep?

"Before Passing Out, junior cadets meet out punishment to their seniors. The idea is to get over any ill-feeling that the juniors might have, because of the intense ragging that the seniors subject them to when they join," I remembered nana saying this.

Uday and Dev belonged to the same Squadron – Golf Squadron. What a strange coincidence it was that the two people I loved the most belonged to the same Squadron.

Looking at the Sudan Block evoked such a feeling of timelessness; I was now standing where I had longed to be. From there we went to the 'Hut of Remembrance.' Here, the names of all the martyred officers who had passed out from the NDA are engraved. Seeing the name of Captain Uday Sharma listed at No. 13, I felt that he was still very much present. Death has never been able to destroy life. Captain Uday Sharma is still very much alive.

It was dusk when we reached the Squadron. "Dev, will this dream of ours remain a dream," I said with a tinge of sadness.

"Mrinalini, this dream has been my only dream. I promise not to live this dream just in my dreams but want to fulfill it in reality. I promise."

When I was leaving for Pune, mummy had become emotional and said, "Who will now go to the NDA from our family? This tradition has ended with Uday."

At the time of the Passing Out Parade, Uday had written to Jaya, "Now that I am passing out from NDA, once we get married, I will bring you to my Squadron. Time will fly and one day we will see our son as a cadet here in the same Squadron and we will come to meet him."

But Uday mama could not fulfill his promise of bringing Jaya to his Squadron. Would Jaya have grown tired of waiting? But Dev had brought me to the same Squadron.

"Mrinalini, you had mentioned that Capt Uday Sharma wanted to bring Jaya ma'am here but could not. But I have fulfilled my promise of bringing you here."

"I am sure, Dev you will fulfill all your promises."

In a moment, I was flooded with many memories – I had performed Uday mama's *shraddh*, met Col and Mrs Mishra. Jaya was a common link between all of us, hence this visit to Pune with Dev. In doing this, I had once again re-lived Uday mama's entire life. But Dev had not wanted me to go to meet Jaya.

"Why are you going to Pune? You could stir up a storm in Jaya ma'am's life after so many years. Why do you want to create ripples in someone's otherwise peaceful existence?" But I was extremely keen to meet Jaya.

Dev said, "Look at their engagement photograph which is in the house and be happy. Please, I beg of you, don't make me a party to your crazy plans."

"Mrs Mishra had said that Jaya wouldn't mind my meeting her, rather she'll be happy that someone so close to Uday has come to look her up," I said in my defence.

Irritated, he said, "Since when have you become interested in socializing that you are going to look up Jaya ma'am?"

"Dev, please come along. How will I find my way in a new place on my own? Even otherwise, I never go anywhere without you."

"Fine. When have I not agreed to whatever you have said? You always do what you want to. God alone knows how many rules I must have broken for your sake. Logic and reason take a back seat when it comes to you. Now don't go about saying that if I don't do this then *tum mera maraa muh dekhoge.*"

Finally, he did come to Pune with me, though rather reluctantly. On reaching Jaya's house, Dev hesitated, "Mrinalini, this is our Unit officer's house. You are going to embarrass me. Have you spoken to Mrs Jaya Kumar, or have you landed up just like that? *Aap kuch bhi kar sakti hain*. Look, the Army has its own protocol, like seeking an appointment before wanting to meet a person. But you have only one rule – 'if there is a rule, it is meant to be broken.'"

Thoroughly irritated, Dev had now started to address me as *'aap'*. To this, I snapped, "First decide whether I am an *aap* or a *tum*. Don't address me as *'aap'* when you are angry. And for your information, I have taken an appointment. Mrs Mishra has also spoken to Mrs Jaya Kumar."

Finally, the moment was here. I was going to meet Jaya after such a long wait. It was she who opened the door. I had always thought of her as Jaya. She recognized me and said, "Please, do come in."

Dev introduced us formally, "Ma'am, I am Major Dev Sharma. Col Kumar and I are from the same Unit. I have met you once in Allahabad."

She immediately replied, "I remember having met you, Major Sharma."

"Ma'am, this is my friend Mrinalini Sharma. She has been wanting to meet you for a long time. She is the daughter of your family friend, Mrs Neeraja Sharma. I will take your leave now as I have some work to do," saying this he left.

Speechless, I kept staring at Jaya for some time. Even after so many years I could easily recognize Uday's Jaya. At that moment, I felt how easy and yet so difficult it must have been to live like this.

"How is Neeraja didi? Its been ages since I met her."

"Mummy remembers you very often. I had met Col and Mrs Mishra in Lucknow and they gave me your address. Ma'am, I have been very eager to meet you for a long time."

"Don't call me ma'am. Don't be so formal. Our families have been friends for long, even though we are meeting for the first time. Daddy and Umakant chacha have been childhood friends. I have known Neeraja didi and jijajee since I was a kid. Once, I happened to meet Neeraja didi in Allahabad as well."

I remained quiet.

I wanted to ask, say and listen to so much, but a strange sadness had started to engulf me. Perhaps both of us were flooded with memories of Capt Uday Sharma. Although I was seeing her for the very first time, I had thought of her and also heard a lot about her.

Would she have treasured all that love with her still? What would have happened to her when Uday mama did not come back? Wouldn't life have ended suddenly for her?

"Mrinalini, I feel a very different kind of joy on meeting you," she said, sipping tea.

Perhaps some old sorrows had now mingled with the present joy. I must have brought back so many haunting memories to her. Time and again I pondered who would have destined this? I wish I could erase it and rewrite it.

With great difficulty I said, "It's been a long time since all this happened. How do you...?" Before I could complete my sentence, she said, "Mrinalini, nothing changes with the mere passage of years, although, yes, something does change. Even though Uday has gone away, he is still very much with me."

"I may be meeting you for the first time, but it does not feel so. I have never seen Uday mama, but he has been with us, for every moment of our lives. You have been with him always and therefore, with us too."

"Today, I am very happy that someone so close to Uday has come to meet me. Relationships might get old or may become distant or get scattered but they don't ever break. It's only time that can test their strength, I am realizing this strength now."

I had seen nana and mummy dwell in the past. Therefore, now, I could realize what Jaya aunty must be going through and started feeling guilty.

"Mummy said to me 'Mrinalini, you were born long after Uday was gone and you haven't even seen him, but you are still so attached to him. Your coming here is an attempt to strengthen old ties.'"

"Aunty, this relationship has always been a part of my existance. Mummy always cherishes relationships and I have learnt this from her. I have re-lived this past so many times with mummy, it's like making one's yesterday a part of one's today and then making a new future out of it."

"There is no escape from the pain of losing dear ones. Even now, after so many years, at times it's hard to believe that Uday will never come back. I still cherish his memories, even today," she said as if talking to herself.

"Aunty, many a times the path may end, but the journey goes on."

"Mrinalini, Uday and I had walked together on so many paths. We had made so many promises and wherever we had walked together I feel those lanes must be still remembering us."

I didn't know what was the predominant emotion in my heart. However, I started telling Jaya aunty about the letters that we had found in Uday mama's belongings.

"Aunty, there were some letter's in Uday mama's trunk – a lot many still unopened letters. Mummy recalls how you used to send many letters packed in a single, large envelope because in those days letters took a long time to reach. Mama would open one letter every Saturday and read it. Many of the letters had remained unopened in the end. They had been lying in the old trunk and mummy often arranges and rearranges them for no apparent reason." I went on, "Last year, I immersed all the letters in the Ganga. Often in life, there are things that remain unsaid sometimes, forever."

Jaya aunty asked, "Where is Uday's Unit now? At that time it was in Himachal. He went via Lucknow on the special train. That was when we met for the last time."

"Aunty, the Unit is now in Ferozepur. Mummy, Shubha, Manu, Dev and I have been there. Mummy wanted to present a memento in Uday mama's memory. People do so much in memory of their loved ones and we hadn't done anything till then. A formal function was organized where we met all the officers of the Unit. Many bygone things came up for discussion and people of the Unit were astonished at my knowledge of the 1962 war. One of the officers complimented me and said, "It looks as if you yourself were present there during the war." Aunty each day, month and year that I have lived with mummy and will keep on living, Uday mama is with us every moment. He was fond of sweets; he loved lighting crackers on Diwali, who all were his friends and where all they went holidaying together—I know virtually everything about him. You know, many years ago he had got a shawl for mummy from Nagaland. My Manu wraps it around herself even now, while sleeping," I kept on speaking.

"When Uday did not come back my life came to a complete stand still. I could not think of any tomorrow. Is time, the best healer? A broken heart does not mend. Even after so many years, time has not been able to fill the void left by Uday. Today, after all these years, I still miss him as much as before. When he did not come back every living moment of my existence was immersed in his thoughts. With every foot step that I heard, it seemed as he was coming. It appeared as if the sun would not rise without Uday. In despair I would call out to him, "Uday, I am so lonely without you and so must you be. Come back for me," tears were streaming down her face.

Then, composing herself she asked, "The CO then, was Col Mehta. Uday used to be Mrs Mehta's favourite youngster. I had met her only once in Lucknow in 1961 when the Unit was moving to Ambala. By the way, who is the CO now?"

"Col Kapoor is the CO."

I recounted, "Aunty, mummy had a premonition that something had happened to Uday mama. She says that on the night of 18th/19th November 1962, she suddenly started weeping in her sleep. She dreamt that a man was walking on the road in front of our house and suddenly a group of 7 or 8 people surrounded him and started beating him mercilessly. The man was fighting very bravely but he fell down, while his attackers started to laugh loudly. By then, papa had woken her up. Terrified, she said, "Something has happened to my Uday." She couldn't say anything further. To this date, she never utters that Uday mama is no more. May be there is a ray of hope that this endless wait will perhaps end some day. Do you know, as per the records, the date of Uday mama's martyrdom is 19th November, 1962."

"Mrinalini, for years everyone hoped and awaited for Uday's return, thinking, he might come back some day. That is why no last rites or any such ceremony was ever performed."

"Aunty, I recently performed Uday mama's *shraddh* at the *sangam* in Allahabad. But mummy still hopes that he may return some day. After the *shraddh,* mummy had said, 'Come let's go to Se-La Pass to meet Uday, just as we are waiting for him to return, who knows he may he may be waiting for us there.'"

"Mummy has never expressed any wish except going to Se-La. But after coming back from there, will her hope of Uday mama returning still be there? This gives her strength. It's only because of this belief she has been able to overcome so many ups and downs in life. This is one hope that consoles her during tough times. Her love for her dear brother is her strength. No matter, reason may tell her that those gone will be gone forever. She draws strength from her hope and moves on." By now it was difficult to maintain my composure but I kept on talking.

"Life is strange – bonds formed over several lives are broken here. The Almighty many a times scatters everything and throws it so far away that it takes many such lives and eons to pick up these pieces and put them back together again. There is nothing, that is left behind is almost impossible to accept. Mrinalini, when you take Neeraja didi to Se-Pa Pass do ask Uday, "Why did you not come back? So many years have gone by, how much longer do we still have to wait?" He had promised me nothing when he left but I have waited for him, all my life. Did he never think of any one of us?" She had started to cry.

Then, as if asking herself, she said, "When the end would have come and in his last moment whom would Uday have thought of? What would have been his last thought? Would he have been able to carry my memories to the next world?" She was now sobbing her heart out.

"Those silent words, that diminishing heart beat would only have called out to Jaya." I thought.

After composing myself, I said, "In that journey from this world to the next, Uday mama would have thought of only one person, "Jaya". He would have carried only your memories with him from, this world. Everything else would have been left behind."

On my way back from Pune, I kept thinking about Uday mama, Jaya aunty, Col Mehta and others. I kept mentally traversing between Se-La Pass, Tawang and Sogia Lake. I had purposely not mentioned my having met Mrs Mehta to Jaya aunty. Both had lost their entire world almost at the same time and I did not want to reconnect Jaya aunty to that past of hers. Mrs Mehta was living her life under the shadow of Col Mehta, but Jaya aunty did not have Uday mama.

I had met Mrs Mehta in Faridabad, after my visit to Uday mama's Unit. She had said, "Once your life is entwined with someone else's, both lives become one. When he does not come back, it becomes impossible to accept this fact. It took me more than three years to come to terms that Col Mehta will never come back. Every footstep would give me hope that Rajan would appear suddenly and say, "Here I am." I had a long life ahead of me. I was barely thirty then. These days, girls are not even married at that age. I brought up my two children pretending to be happy when there was no happiness around. I cried many a times without shedding a tear. I am a *fauji's* wife, very strong willed. There were moments of weakness when I felt that I would crumple. It felt as if there was nothing left in my life."

Trying hard not to sob she continued, "I did everything I could and in the same manner as Rajan would have done had he been there. The void of his absence will always be there, but there is no question of us being separated. We are still together and will continue to be."

I saw many old photographs with Mrs Mehta. In one of them, Uday mama was dressed as a Sikh, this was when he had been to Goa. "Mrinalini, did you know that Col Mehta's *Paltan* is the one to whom, the Portuguese had surrendered in December 1961? Rajan had been called for an urgent conference to the Division Headquarters in November, 1961. The advance party had moved to Goa via Belgaum in the beginning of December, 1961. The D-Day came soon. The Portuguese Commander-in-Chief and their Naval Chief had surrendered. What a proud moment it was for all of us! We were all still under the hangover of the liberation of Goa and were in the process of settling down in the peace station when the call came."

I saw Jaya aunty's photograph, also with her.

"I met Jaya later on. When Uday showed me her photo, I liked her so much that I kept the photo with me."

She was remembering each and every thing associated with Uday mama.

"Uday had been recognized by his ruck-sack which was inscribed with US. There was nothing else left of him with which he could have been identified. 5 officers and about 60 to 70 other ranks who fought with thousands of Chinese. Rajan had said, "All of you quietly slip away in different directions," but all of them had said in unison, "Sir, we live together and we die together." All of them fought valiantly and went down fighting."

"What would have happened at the end?" I could not resist asking, the question which had haunted me since childhood.

"Nobody can tell what would have actually happened in the end. The war diary or the Unit Digest do not have any entry beyond 18th November 1962. I tried hard to find out. I even traced out the orderly in the hospital who was the lone eye witness to that fateful night," she continued sadly.

"Aunty, what did that orderly tell you?" I was desperate to know.

Mrs Mehta said, "That orderly bid final adieu to all the five officers. He stayed back for three days in the bitterly cold weather, without food or water, waiting for the Chinese to retreat. Then he buried them in the snow. He had said, 'At least this dignity was due to the *sahabs*.' He himself was badly wounded and both his legs had to be amputated because of frostbite. It was only after meeting this orderly that I had started to slowly accept the reality that Col Mehta will never come back. Was it easy to accept this? Not at all. It was like fighting a war with one's own self. Despite knowing this truth, I have tightly shut all doors of reasoning for all these years."

"Ma'am, nana had suffered a nervous breakdown after this. Mummy had a tough time consoling him. It was almost impossible to console him for he would always wait for Uday mama to come back. Then one day something strange happened. Nana had a client called Hari Singh whom he had successfully defended in many criminal cases. He had come to meet nana and had said, "Why are you grieving for your son? He has met such a glorious end that I envy him. Look at me, I have lived for so long and have only managed to be labelled a criminal. Your son is a martyr. He had lived his allotted number of days in this world and so he had to go. Had he not been in the war, he would have gone anyway. May be after a brief illness, from which even the best doctor would not have been able to save him.

"Mummy had been stunned to hear this and thought that Hari Singh had had it. But to everyone's astonishment nana completely broke down and wept. After that, mummy and nana had started to come to terms with reality, somewhat."

"Though time is the best healer, who has ever been able to rise above time?" Mrs Mehta remarked sadly.

"I had met Col Mishra who explained to me in detail about the battle in defence of Se-La Pass. Col Mehta and his brave men this is how Col Mishra remembered them. Eventually, about a hundred soldiers of ours had taken on thousands of Chinese."

"No Mrinalini, not even a hundred. By the morning of 19th November, only a handful—may be just 10 to 20 of our men were left who fought the Chinese. The Chinese war strategy was based on the human wave technique. They would attack in innumerable numbers and would continue to attack until they captured the place. They attacked in such huge, unimaginable numbers. Ordinarily during war one defender can take on 3 attackers, in extreme conditions this ratio can go upto 1:10. But if one defender had to take on 40 to 50 attackers or more, you can imagine the outcome. But they all fought valiantly till the end and when the ammunition was over, then they even took on the enemy with their bayonets," Mrs Mehta sighed.

9

In the beginning of November, 2001, Dev had left for training. Hence, when Operation Parakram started, I was relieved that normally his training would not be cancelled.

I was in Delhi at Shubha's place in December, 2001. I was to return soon but stayed back because she wanted me to. We were shopping that day in Noida, when the call came. Dev spoke in his usual style, "Darling, I am missing you a lot. I am coming the day after. 'When are you coming? It has been such a long time,' you have literally killed me, by saying this again and again."

"Really, Dev?" I could not believe my ears.

He laughed and said "Mem saab, the course has been cancelled and I have to report at Jammu immediately."

I was dumbstruck.

Shubha and I went to receive Dev. The train was delayed by 4 hours. He was to stay only for the night and had to leave for Jammu, the next morning.

Whole night we kept awake. We had spent countless nights like this, in the past. I was too numb to say anything but I managed to say, "Dev, come back soon. You have got to come back for me. Forget days, each moment seems longer than a day. I will wait for you to come back soon."

Dev remained silent.

"My fears haunt me. I dread reading news papers. No matter how much Shubha tries to reason with me, but because I have seen everyone waiting endlessly for Uday mama, that I lose all confidence in myself." I shuddered with an unknown fear.

Dawn was approaching when Dev said, "I promise that I will come back to you. But what have you thought about us, Mrinalini? How long will we keep meeting and then departing, again like this? Your wait will end but what about my long wait?"

I kept quiet and did not know what to say. It was true that my life would have no meaning without Dev. We spent many such nights together but Dev had always respected our relationship.

I had lovingly asked, many a times, "Dev, you must be the only person in this world to have loved me like this."

"I love you so much that I can never even think of doing anything against your wishes. The day you come to me, believing fully and completely in our love, having absolute faith in me, then only... not until then, never." He would always reply confidently, full of love.

I have cried on Dev's shoulder through the night often, which would upset him. He would take me in his arms, "Mrinalini, stop sobbing like this. This makes me question my very existence. If I cannot keep you happy and you have to sob your heart out like this, then my very existence is meaningless. Tell me, what is it that you want? Please stop crying. It upsets me no end. If you are not happy then nothing has any meaning for me."

"Dev, will you always be there for me? Will you always love me like this? Mrinalini's life begins and ends with Dev."

He would laugh and say, "I, Major Dev Sharma IC No. ... swear that I will love you, Mrinalini the most and will keep on doing so forever." I would quarrel with him, and ask jokingly, "If you love me the most, then whom do you love a little less? *Maar dalungi,* Major Dev Sharma, if you ever dare to love anybody else, even a little."

"*Yaar,* let me love somebody else, may be just a little, once in a while. If I love somebody else, though I will not but it is better to have your permission." He would pull my leg.

"Dev, when will you stop loving me?"

Whenever I would ask him jokingly, his answer would always be, "May be a life time, I will never stop loving you" he would answer full of conviction, resting his head on my shoulder.

When Dev was about to leave for Jammu in the morning, Shubha put a *tikka* on his forehead as a send off. When she tried to hand over some money to him, he felt a bit odd.

"When mummy hands over money, after putting *tikka,* you joke about inflation. Why is it so odd to take money from me? When you send someone off, after handing money, he is suppose to come back home, sooner," she smiled and said.

"Dev, time has flown by in a jiffy and now you are leaving. *Mujhe choo kar kaho* that you will come back soon," I said.

"Time is strange. Before you realize that time has come, it has already gone. *Tumhe choo kar kahta hoon* that I will come back to my Mrinalini and my Manu very soon."

The days were flying by once again. When Dev is not around, the clock moves so slowly. It's difficult to pass time. It's tough to live through each moment without him. But today time seemed to be in a real hurry.

While leaving, Dev held my hand and said, "See you."

He would never turn and look back, while going. He would say, "If I turn and look back at you, I would not be able to go. My feet would compel me to walk back towards you."

Even now, I silently watched him leave.

I continued to live in a strange void for many days. Even after Dev had left, his presence could be felt in the room. That empty cup of tea, that lingering smell of aftershave on the pillow and that wet towel, flung carelessly on the back of the chair, would all remind me of him.

Dev had travelled beyond Jammu in a convoy. He had called up on the way, "Look after yourself. There is a crowd at the PCO. I can't be selfish. Everybody out here is waiting for his turn. I shall speak to you again, very soon."

After the recall, all the Army phone connections had been cut off. For the next three weeks there was no news of Dev. These three weeks seemed like 300 years. Then one evening, he had called up in my office. The line was disturbed.

"Where we have been put up, there is a cremation ground, right in front. Today itself a body has been cremated."

"Dev, is this something to tell me? It scares me even more, talk of something nice."

"I had gone out yesterday and we were crossing the rope bridge which was shaking violently in the wind. I was reminded of you— how you would have shrieked in fear and caught hold of me, it would have been great. You are scared of so many things—rats, lizards, cockroaches, dogs etc." he was teasing me.

"Do you keeping making a list of things that scare me?"

Dev had mentioned that there was a very old gurudwara near the post. He would often go and sit there. He would pray, "God Almighty keep Mrinalini happy. Let there be no sorrows in her life and give all my happiness to her."

The old *granthi* would see him praying every day. One day he had asked, "Sahab, you come here every day. For whom do you pray with such devotion and what is it that you ask for?"

"There is someone, very dear to me rather the dearest to me. I pray for her."

After a few days, he returned back to the Unit.

When, in winter I had sent a pretty Rajasthani *razai* for Dev, Shubha had teased me so much. "Poor Major Dev Sharma would have frozen in the cold winter of Kashmir but for this pretty but rather thin Rajasthani *razai!*"

Whenever Dev travelled to other posts, he would always carry the *razai* with him.

By now, the *razai* had turned black from the smoke of the *bukhari*. His *sahayak* would wonder looking at the *razai* if it was of any use any longer? He had been shouted at by Dev once, when asked if the *razai* would be taken to the post.

Ever since, the *razai* was the first item that the *sahayak* would pack.

It was winters and time was moving slowly. After snowfall, a strange quiet would descend.

Once Dev had said over the phone, "Mrinalini, the roar of the fast flowing Jhelum down the valley is unable to soothe my restless heart even for a moment."

Changing the subject, I had asked, "It must be very cold there by now?"

"Darling, it's awfully cold and it has snowed, but it seems as if a full moon has risen in my room even though it's actually an *amavas,* because you are here with me. I can sense your presence all around me."

"Dev, how romantic!"

"The warmth of love has engulfed my soul, and now I long for you even more." He would sit alone and think, "When we are married, and I take Mrinalini to my village, the women there will surely make fun of her English and she too, would not understand their language. She will then ask, "What are they saying in their language, Dev? I hope they are not mocking me?"

When I had visited his village, Dev had challenged me, "If you go and touch that cow over there, I will give you 500 rupees."

"The cow will bite me," I had said, and everyone had laughed! Amma had said, "Mrinalini, cows kick and dogs bite!"

And I had gone with Dev's bhabhi and touched the cow. I was now hell-bent on sqeezing the money out of him.

"Give me my 500 rupees, you *kanjoos*."

"Now that you have labelled me a *kanjoos,* why should I part with my money? You are not going to get anything. Anyway, you did not go alone but took bhabhi along."

The upstairs room in the house was Dev's.

He would think that when he would call out to Mrinalini every now and then, amma and bhabhi would eventually get fed-up and send her upstairs. He had taken great pains to do up the room. The mattress had been laid down on the floor with the music system close by. On the wall was the picture of a girl that Mrinalini had brought when she had come to meet him for the first time. The girl appeared to be lost in someone's thoughts. He had joked and said, "Is she lost in my thoughts? And that clock, ...

"Dev this clock chimes every hour. I have got this so that it reminds you of me, every hour. Always remember me, don't ever forget me. This clock will never let you forget me." Neither of us had realized the depth of my words then.

Why this solitary existence? Dev would think. The saying, *'bin gharni ghar bhoot ka dera,'* was so true. The mere thought of Mrinalini would fill him up with such happiness, even when he was sitting all alone amidst snow-clad mountains. Though there was nothing in this barrenness, the thought of Mrinalini would make the entire surroundings beautiful.

Any sudden sound in the stillness would remind him of the time when she had once arrived in Allahabad all of a sudden, without informing him. Whenever loneliness seemed to overcome him, he had so many pleasant memories of her to recall and weave many new dreams around them. Many a time, he would start talking to Mrinalini – "Mrinalini, the snow has started to melt now and the entire place is covered with lovely flowers."

"Don't you miss me amidst so many flowers?"

"Mrinalini, I have covered the entire place with flowers, but it seems as if my destiny has only a long wait. I do not know how long I have to keep waiting."

"Dev, I have been holding your hand and my destiny has become one with yours."

Last year, on our way back from Varanasi, Shubha and I had gone to Dev's village. This had sent tongues wagging, and a rumour that Dev was getting married soon, and his city-bred fiancé had come to take a look at her *sasural*, was rife! The next day, people had enquired of amma, "You've fixed Dev's marriage and we do not even know about it?"

What could amma have replied except saying, "Mrinalini is just a friend of Dev's."

In the village, friendship between a man and a woman was unheard of, and some people gossiped that we were probably already married.

"Mrinalini, here in the village everybody thinks that

you are my wife. Why don't you come and take care of me? In the village the wives cook, clean, wash, do *sasuma's seva,* take care of the husband, keep him happy and have half a dozen kids. And mind you, do not call me by my name here. Your habit of saying 'Dev' at the beginning and end of every sentence will not be appreciated at all. Once I leave, you will wait for me and look out for the postman, just like all the other wives."

"Am I suppose to look after you? Why? Are you a child? You have made out a very nice role model for me. Shall I tell everyone here that you can wash clothes better than me, you can chop vegetables properly, you can shop well for groceries, and when I get tired and my feet ache, you can massage them very well."

Dev would often ponder that amma was so fond of Mrinalini. If only he had met her earlier. 'If only,' had been the cause of all woes in his life but not anymore. This 'if only' may have been significant for amma as well as for Mrinalini. It was absolutely insignificant for him.

"Look at Mrinalini, how tall and beautiful she is. She has a good job but is not at all arrogant. What else do you want in a '*bahu*'?" amma would often ask happily.

"Amma, do you know what a lot Mrinalini spends on clothes and jewellery? She is capable of blowing away my entire salary in a day. She cannot do household work and just look at her crooked nose? If she does not like something, she starts making a fuss. She is not going to stay here with you anyway. And kids? She will refuse to have more than one," he would say.

Amma was very fond of Mrinalini and she was determined to have a daughter-in-law like her. She would say, "If Mrinalini dresses up well, so what? She is beautiful. She herself earns so much. Which *bahu* does household work these days? Children too are God's gift. As for the crooked nose, if she puts on a nose ring that would look pretty."

"Amma had an answer to everything. He wanted to tell that Mrinalini is the one I love but was unable to say so. Will she be acceptable to you, amma?"

By February, the phone lines had been restored. But still it was difficult to get through and on top of that often Dev would not be available. Many a times he would be out and when he would call there would be disturbance. The operator would often have to interrupt in between. I would be, upset and scared. I spent restless and sleepless nights. Dev would say, "Dream of our life together, close your eyes and think of our love."

One night when the phone suddenly rang, I was really frightened by the late night call fearing something untoward. Before I could even say 'Hello' I could hear Dev humming at the other end.

Hum tum na hum tum rahe ab, kuch aur hi ban gaye hain...

I was reassured to find him in a real carefree and jolly mood, but still I told "Dev, please don't do this again. I almost died. Do you know what time is it? It's 3 a.m. How come you are calling at this hour?"

"Darling, I called you in such a romantic mood, thinking that you will be overjoyed to hear my voice. But it appears that you are actually scared."

He was drunk that night and had become very emotional. The absence of Mrinalini was now tormenting him.

He would be tempted to ignore all social norms and bring Mrinalini to be with him forever. Why is she so much bothered by the society and its norms?

"Mrinalini, shall I tell you how I felt after hearing your voice? It felt as if you are right here with me."

During the call, Dev's Commanding Officer had also come. He did not ask Dev anything then but the next day it became the talk of the Unit that when the radio relay is shut down at midnight, then how could this call have been made?

I had once asked Dev if he missed me in Kashmir, "Don't you long for me in the beautiful valleys of Kashmir." At that time he did not say anything but I received a letter after a few days.

Mrinalini darling,

> The place where we are is, surrounded by mountains. On a full moon night, the moon rises at around six in the evening but is hidden behind the mountains. I keep sitting alone in the darkness while the moon illuminates the mountains all around. After a long wait, suddenly the full moon appears over the mountains. The snow capped peaks of the mountains look heavenly.

Do you know that the moon within two to three hours spreads its shine upon the snow capped peaks milky white. But who knows how long I will have to wait? When will you come and illuminate my life?

Do you know what do I do? You are sure to get upset when you hear this – I keep sitting out in the cold and keep on drinking the whole night. You cannot imagine how much I miss you and long for you. I ask myself, "Mrinalini, when will you come in my life, forever? How long do I have to wait—how long will I keep dreaming of you?"

Yours only,

Dev

On reading the letter, I was filled with pride, but at the same time I was also filled with deep sadness.

Since Bimal from Dev's unit had started to man the PCO, it had become easier to call up. He would connect my calls immediately. No matter where Dev was, he would manage to find him. If someone else was talking on the line he would ask him to hang up saying *"phone jaldi rakhiye, sahab ka phone hai. Mem saab full rate par call kar rahi hain."*

The call would go via many exchanges and Bimal would be after each one to connect the call. He would tell me, "Mem saab I will connect the call and, you please hang up and call after two minutes. If I don't answer take it that the line is busy still."

Those days Dev would go out every day in the morning and get back around four in the afternoon. One day when I had called up at five in the evening, Bimal had at once transferred the call to the other exchange but the operator there said, "Major Sharma has not returned yet."

At this I got worried and said, "Bimal, as soon as Major Sharma returns ask him to call me."

I would be waiting for Dev to return and till he would come back I would not be able to do anything. That day Bimal came to know Dev had returned by four as usual.

Bimal complained to Dev, "Sahab, the operators at the next exchange do not connect the call when mem saab calls up. She often calls up at full rate and they lie to her that you have not returned. She in return gets upset. Today also they did the same."

That day I had seen Dev angry for the first time. He told Bimal to call me up. The call went through immediately, while he was hauling up the operator at the other exchange, in between Bimal was telling, "Sahab, mem saab is on the line."

I could clearly hear Dev shouting with such rage for such a small thing!

"Bimal, put me on to Major Sharma."

Dev was shouting at the operator of the other exchange, "Whenever in future mem saab calls, you will find me from wherever I am and put her call through to me. You good for nothing fellow."

I interrupted, "Dev, you have come back after a long day, you must be tired. Calm down."

"I was getting worried so I asked Bimal to make you call up as soon as you returned. I am sorry. Please don't get angry."

"Darling, no one should dare to misbehave with my mem saab. In future this scoundrel will behave himself and not fool around with me."

In March, Bimal went on leave he had informed me.

"Mem saab, I am going on leave. I will tell my replacement to connect your calls."

It was difficult to get leave. Generally a week's leave was granted but Bimal, after a lot of pleading had managed two weeks' leave.

A month had passed but I had not heard Bimal's familiar voice. When I had asked Dev, he laughingly replied "How come you are so concerned about Bimal? He has gone home and is not fighting a war. He will over stay and to top it will make a million excuses *mar gaya tha, lut gaya tha, barbaad ho gaya tha*—my mother was sick, my father was sick. He might also end up telling that one or two of his relatives had died. He will not admit that he was honeymooning with his wife."

"Don't be so crude, Dev. Bimal is not given any family accommodation and you give leave only once a year or may be once in two years. If he told the truth would you grant him some more leave?"

Bimal had returned after 40 days. I was relieved to hear his familiar voice. He had made the same old routine excuses in the Unit. He was afraid to be marched up. Many a times without even having met a person, one forms a bond of some sort. I had decided to plead Bimal's case and called up

Dev, "Dev, will you agree to do something for me? Just once? I will never request anything from you ever again."

"I have always agreed to whatever you have said and will always do so darling. But why is it that you are almost pleading. I can't make out if the sun now rising or is it setting?"

"The sun will always rise in the East and set in the West," saying this I had put the phone down.

Actually, I was feeling awkward to plead Bimal's case as the rules of the Army are very strict. Was I trying to emotionally exploit Dev? I would sympathise with Bimal. He would call me Sharma sahab's mem saab with a lot of respect. Without having met me he showed so much concern. Finally, I could not help calling up Dev again, "Dev if you love me, then please grant me this."

"What is it that you want, Mrinalini? Why don't you tell me straight away what is it that you desire? For the past two days you have been calling up and pleading for something. Order me, I am all yours to command. Take my life, if that is what you want, I just don't like that Major Dev Sharma's wife-to-be is pleading for something," he had asked me lovingly.

"Dev, please don't march up, Bimal." Saying that, I quickly put the phone down.

Dev had called up the next day, he said in a serious tone, "Bimal has been a give a tough punishment. Go on extended leave, enjoy the company of your wife and to top it, have mem saab to make recommendation for you! What else did you expect?"

I had got annoyed and said, "Dev, if you had let Bimal off

what would have happened? If you have to punish someone, punish me instead. What will he think that sahab does not listen mem saab at all?"

Then I got agitated and said, "I may even die here. What difference would that make to you? Your world will remain the same."

"Do you really know me? This is what you think? When you have assured Bimal that he would not be marched up then how could I have punished him? I let him off and four others along with him. What luck? The scoundrel impressed you so much by flattering you over the phone that you made me let him off. And look at me, even after such a long time who cares for me?" He kept on laughing.

"Thank you, Dev. I love you so much. I compelled you to do something wrong. Never again will I ask you to do anything like this. Bimal is the one who takes me a step closer to you. Thats why he is so special," I said cheerfully.

The winters were over and after the new year came Holi. I had sent *gulaal* for Dev. The post office guy had created so much trouble for sending that small packet of *gulaal*. He even labelled me as a possible woman terrorist. The scented, herbal *gulaal* was liked very much by everyone in the Unit. The Commanding Officer while putting *gulaal* on everyone had said, "Sharma's would-be, could-be mem saab has sent such nice *gulaal*."

Then he had asked Dev, "Sharma you get so many phone calls and letters. When are you getting married?" At which Dev had just laughed. It was true that there was no place in India where he had been posted and I had not sent him a letter, called him up, or had not sent something for him, whenever somebody was going there. When during leave he would go to his village, I would call him. If someone else answered the phone, I would immediately disconnect, feeling awkward. Sometimes, I would have Shubha make the call. Amma would get annoyed and say, "Only women ring up Dev. No man ever calls him up."

"Amma, all beautiful girls in town are trying to woo your son, though only a few of them ring up."

Irritated, she said, "Then why don't you get married to one of them?"

Dev had no answer to this question.

10

In May 2002, Dev was coming back to Delhi. Shubha and I had gone to the airport to receive him. The Army special courier from Srinagar was, as usual late and had not landed until 3 pm. Due to security reasons there was no information being given. Anxious and impatient we had taken innumerable rounds of the arrival lounge. We had been to every tea and coffee stall. Finally, tired, I sat down on a sofa. They had not announced the arrival of the courier yet, when we would see the *faujis* walking in their combat uniforms, only then could we know that the flight had finally arrived. Shubha beckoned me "Come." I went ahead but there was no sign of Dev for the next half an hour.

"May be he has stayed back in Srinagar to finish some work."

"Dev had called me from the airport in the morning. Mrinalini, control your anger. He is coming after a long time," irritated Shubha had said. I looked away ignoring her completely.

I recalled how when Dev had to come on leave in March from Kashmir there was no convoy that day. His programme had been finalized at the last moment. Prior to this, he was unable to come as his leave had been cancelled. I had been really very upset then. He had not disclosed the real reason to me for not coming. He had just said, "Mrinalini, I am unable to come. I am sorry."

He had purposely not revealed the real reason for his not coming. Had he told it to, me I would have been very upset. Dev took up convoy protection duty for months together while other officers avoided it. It was not easy to travel a 100 kms or so in the day and return the very next day. He did not refuse convey protection duty at all. Instead, he would say, "Mrinalini, your prayers and love will always protect me. I will always be safe."

"Why do you always take up this convoy protection duty?" Whenever I would ask, he had the same old reply, "Every afternoon on reaching Srinagar, I get to talk to you from a PCO and again the next morning before I start back. Otherwise, its difficult to speak over the Army phone. Our exchange is out of order for weeks together. When its not out of order, it's shut down because of lightening or bad weather." I would be speechless to this reply.

When he had come earlier, there was no convoy that day. He covered those 100 kms by taking lift in Army and civil vehicles. He had managed to reach Srinagar airport just in time for the flight. When I learnt of this, my heart almost stopped beating for a moment.

"Dev, this is madness. How can you be so reckless?"

"Love and madness go hand-in-hand. Why are you so scared? See for yourself nothing has happened to me. I am standing fit and fine in front of you, all of my 5 feet and 9 inches, Major Dev Sharma at your service ma'am, all yours to command," he had said lovingly.

This chain of thoughts was interrupted when, after a long wait, I saw Dev. He waved and Shubha, too, waved back. I happily rushed forward and hugged him.

"Look Shubha, being apart for five months has its own pluses. There is no usual nagging – 'don't drink so much'... 'don't do this'... 'don't do that' – in turn you end up getting a loving embrace. I hope I have landed up in the right place?'" He then jokingly said to a stranger standing nearby, "Is this Delhi?" Then touching his nose to mine, he said, "Darling, I missed you so much. Are we going to Dehradun tomorrow?" "Yes" I replied with joy.

I had always wanted to see IMA and RIMC. But I had decided to go there only with Dev. We had started in the morning and had stopped at Haridwar that night. The entire night we kept remembering old times. When Dev's unit was in Allahabad, I had stopped at a jewelers and had asked, "Dev what will you buy for me?"

"I'll buy you *payals*." He said to the jeweller "Look at these beautiful feet. Please show us some beautiful *payals* befitting them."

After looking at innumerable pairs, at last he selected one. "You don't have a pair that can adorn these beautiful feet, but this will do as she likes it."

Dev always admires my feet, "Mrinalini what delicate, beautiful feet you have. *Maine to bas apna dil hi bicha diya hai inke neeche.*"

"Dev do you remember when last year in Allahabad, we had a fight?" I teased him.

"What fight? With whom? And when? I don't remember," he said.

"Last year we had planned to go to Delhi. The date had also been decided, but at the last moment, for some reason you had declined to come."

And, when I had asked him why he wouldn't come even though he had himself decided the date, he had still not relented. Irritated, I had finally said, "Do whatever you want. I don't care whether you come or not. I won't die if you don't come."

"Why should you die, *aap par marne wale to hum hain,*" he had said.

"Why do you fight with me, Dev?"

"I am not fighting. If I cannot accompany you, it does not mean that I am fighting. You know who fights," he had said looking at me.

"Why would you fight, Mr Innocent?"

When he still didn't reply, I had got annoyed and said, "You have not said your favourite dialogue 'okay see you darling'."

"Thank God, I am still a darling," he had remarked with a hint of sadness.

When I had returned from Allahabad, I had not spoken to him for three days. He had called up on the fourth day, "I am coming tomorrow, on my way to Delhi."

When I remained silent, he said, "Will you come to receive me? Even if you don't, I'll come home. If you do not still speak to me, I will return to Allahabad."

"How can you say that? Won't I come to receive your even though I am annoyed. I wait for you every moment. Have you ever waited for me like this?"

On the way back from the station, Dev stopped at a florist. "I want *rajnigandha*," I started picking out the slender white stems.

"Keep all the flowers that you have in the car," saying this he handed over the car keys to the florist.

"Dev, where will I keep all these flowers? These roses don't look fresh and these tulips must be awfully expensive." Though I said this, I was brimming with happiness. He had quietly paid the florist, and holding my hand, walked out of the shop.

"Dev, you love me so much, and that is what has given me the world. Suddenly, I remembered nana's words, 'God is a great leveller. Wherever He leaves a dirth, He compensates it many fold with something much more beautiful.' Dev's coming into my life was a befitting proof of this."

We had kept talking all night and in the morning we had left for Dehradun. That afternoon Dev took me to IMA. First, we walked around the entire campus and then he took me to the room where he had stayed during his first term and then to the room where he had stayed during the last term.

It was June and preparations for the upcoming, Passing Out Parade were in full swing and all the youngsters were busy.

While passing by the obstacle training area, I had asked, "It must be very difficult to cross this. Isn't it? I wouldn't be able to."

"Darling, we have to work so hard in order to become officers. I have never got anything in life without toiling hard for it. Many a times not even then, I am not that lucky."

At the Chatwood building, seeing the 'Final Step' brought back many memories. I had heard about Uday mama's Passing Out Parade. In December, 1957 he would have crossed this very 'Final Step' and would have become an officer. In January, 1958 he had reported at his Unit.

At the Passing Out Parade, Uday mama and Jaya would have begun to dream about their beautiful future together. "I am so happy right now that you are with me," Uday mama would have reiterated his love for Jaya.

"Uday, this one moment of happiness fulfils my quest for all future moments of happiness," Jaya would have said something like this.

"Where are you? What are you engrossed in?" Dev had asked.

"Dev, I suddenly thought of Uday mama. What did you think when you crossed the 'Final Step'. What dream you had then? Did you think of the love that would come in your life. I was not in your life then but I would love to be associated with some dream of yours that you would have had then."

"I had become an officer one day right here, on crossing this 'Final Step'. Mrinalini, I had a beautiful dream at that time. And now, this moment with you has given me another beautiful dream."

I had become sad as I knew that every *'fauji'* dreams of that moment when, his son would cross the 'Final Step' and become an officer.

Dev had quietly taken me in his arms and I had started to cry.

I had very rightly guessed his dream. Dev had said, "Every officer starts to dream about the future right here. The dream of seeing his son becoming an officer and then being commissioned in his own Unit—it's a proud moment, Mrinalini. But many a times, dreams remain just that, dreams. Yours and mine, our dream, will you fulfill it?"

"Dev, dreams do turn into reality. Where there are no dreams people perish." I had quietly said.

"What are you telling me so lovingly, darling?" he had asked.

"In IMA, wherever I went, everyone thought of me as Dev's wife. Often that which is not real is far more beautiful than what is real. The dream that I had always cherished in my heart, that which was not actually real had given me so much joy."

From the gate of IMA, Dev had called up the adjutant of RIMC and had taken an appointment for the next day.

Next morning on reaching RIMC, Dev remained seated in the car and asked me to go in on my own. On my insisting he said, "Mem saab, I am not from RIMC. You will get a lot of attention there. There is a strong bonding and affinity amongst the Rimcoleans. I am a simple clod who went to a village school. I will be completely out of place amongst you and your Rimcoleans. Even today, this is the premium institution for joining the Army."

I told Dev, "I have been hearing a lot about Uday mama's stint at RIMC. Mummy still remembers each and every detail, as if it was only yesterday."

"Dev, Uday mama was at RIMC from 1948 to 1953. Mummy still remembers his roll number at RIMC, his date of commissioning, his IC number and his date of reporting at the Unit."

Mummy had said, "Just before Uday was about to join NDA, Nargis and Raj Kapoor's 'Awara' had been released in Dehradun. Your mama paid dearly for wanting to watch Nargis in a swim suit. When he had gone to the theatre, the Adjutant of RIMC along with his wife was sitting right behind. What punishment – guess – did he get? He had to walk around entire RIMC with 40 kgs tied to his back. He was in great pain for weeks after, that. When he had come home on leave, bruises were still visible on his back."

By then, I had walked towards the Adjutant's office. Major Rajinder Singh, the Adjutant welcomed me warmly. The board, displaying the names of war heroes had Captain Uday Sharma's name on it.

I had never even for a single moment in my life forgotten Uday mama. I had cherished so many memories of him since childhood. On mere mention of Capt Uday Sharma's roll number and Ranjit Section, his entire record had been pulled out within minutes and placed before me. It contained the entire details about Uday mama—things like the subjects he was good at and also those at which he wasn't, the fee sent by nana, the trips on which he had gone etc. The familiar hand written letters from nana reminded me of the letters that he had regularly written to mummy after papa had passed away.

Nana and mummy had faced life's ups and downs, together. God had tested them a lot. Nani, then Uday mama and their papa, each loss was bigger than life itself and so many of them, one after the other. An ordinary person could not have survived, there surely must have been some divine force that had kept them going. Both of them kept consoling each other and time moved on. Mummy very rightly says, *Dard ka rishte bada atoot hota hai.* When we live through difficult and testing times with someone, then a very close unbreakable bond is formed. In true sense a *dard ka rishta* always remains in your heart, it never dies. Mummy has always been very strong even after nana had passed away, she single handedly kept looking after each one of us.

After having tea in the Adjutant's office I had moved on to see Ranjit Section, where in 1948 an eleven year-old boy Uday Sharma had joined. He had moved out of his home all alone for the very first time.

"Initially, Uday would pine for home. He missed amma and me a lot and would often cry. Amma always said, 'We have only one son, There is so much land and property. What is the need to send him to the Army?' But your nana was determined to send Uday in the Army."

Major Singh had got up to escort me around RIMC, "Ma'am, I will show you around."

"I'll manage, Major Singh."

However, he had insisted and came along. There were children playing around.

Once upon a time, Uday mama would also have been playing around like this. He would have spent so much time walking these very paths, sitting under these very trees, and must have made many friends here. On seeing the dormitories in Ranjit section, I thought that he might have cried hiding his face in the pillows when he would have missed home. He would have written letters to his Neeraja didi, sitting at one of these very tables.

On growing up, he would have experienced the very first emotions of love for Jaya somewhere here.

Dev had been waiting outside in the car. "I have a friend with me", I told Major Singh. Dev had come out of the car. Meanwhile, two other officers had also joined us. They asked Dev, "Have you come on leave? I believe all leave has been cancelled and everyone has been recalled. Anyway, enjoy yourself until you are hear from the Unit. Have a good time." On hearing this, I got upset.

"Dev, will you go back one again? Am I only destined to be away from you and keep on waiting? Will loneliness be my only companion? Will memories be my only comfort?"

I had become totally numb on hearing about the recall. I bade good bye to Major Singh and Dev and I started back immediately. On our way back to the guest house, there was absolute silence. Now I wasn't even able to cry. Since childhood, I would become silent whenever there was a situation in which I did not know what to do or how to find a way out.

Loneliness had started to engulf me. Who would know the pain of loneliness better than me, I was battling this very loneliness, when Dev had suddenly come into my life and had filled all voids. His love had given me all the strength to hold myself together. Now, whenever difficult times would come his love always gave me the confidence and strength to deal with them. Will the future take me back to those dark old days once again? This love, this togetherness; without any label of a formal relationship had brought us together till here. If Dev were to go now, when will he return? While awaiting his return I could barely sleep, all the time waiting and longing for him to come back.

Dev, was gazing at the distant sky, through the window. Perhaps he was thinking, "Mrinalini, what should we name this love of ours? What name should we give this beautiful relationship? I am like the person whose life is full of love, but he cannot talk about it. What would he have said? He would wait to shout from the roof tops. 'I love Mrinalini. I want to marry her and set-up a home with her.' I want to live every moment, every day, every single breath of my life with her. I cannot think of how each moment, each day, week, month, year will go by without her."

Dev, later told me what he had been thinking then at that time in Dehradun. Days gone by, the past hurts, questions that society would ask, the answers to these which Mrinalini has been hesitating and avoiding. What should be done? How would one resolve these? Whats our destiny? Wish that this long wait was a dream. Then at least it would have been over by the time one woke up. How long do we battle with this society? Blaming God was of no use. He would often wonder why he had not met Mrinalini earlier. Many a times he had thought that there are some paths that are endless and one has to keep on walking forever. He was unable to decide, whether the destiny had been kind to him or not? The truth is that he has to live his life with Mrinalini forever.

Today, where he stands with Mrinalini, there are thousands of paths on which they can happily walk together.

He has Mrinalini and her love. He has wanted nothing more in life. How does her past matter? She is unnecessarily perturbed because of her past. He will now not go back to the Unit without making this relationship formal.

He now has to live for Mrinalini, for Manu and himself. He will no longer go by the norms of the society. He will definitely come back to his Mrinalini. This love will always protect him. He has complete faith in himself and this love.

"Mrinalini, let's go." We packed and left for Delhi. He had now given me no time to think or ask any questions.

But for the recall, this journey would have been so pleasant. The silence between us had become unbearable. After living through winters all by myself now that the summers were here, perhaps I will have to suffer the same loneliness once again. Before I could be together with him, he had to go back to the Unit. "Mrinalini darling, by the time the rains will come. I would have joined you once again. Now stop crying." He was thinking of his favourite *Mausam aayenge jayenge....*

"Dev, do you know what had happened? Uday mama had gone one day like this and.... Promise me that you will come back – *mujhe choo kar vada karo*. Without you, I have no existence." I had said with a heavy heart.

My crying would always upset Dev. In the initial days of our relationship, whenever I would cry, he would say, "Mrinalini, why do you cry so much?" My crying had started to become unbearable for him.

"Mrinalini, I promise that I will always come back for you and my sweet Manu. You have created a ghost for yourself. If Capt Uday Sharma did not come back, it does not mean that I am not going to come back. When will you get over this fear? Trust me; your love will always bring me back safely."

His words did not comfort me and I kept on crying during the entire journey back to Delhi.

We had reached Delhi by evening. Shubha, on seeing my swollen eyes asked, *"Kya hua?"*

"I have been recalled. The leave has been cancelled. Look how big and lovely her swollen eyes look. Darling, do not love me so much that I may not want to go back. People will taunt you that Major Dev Sharma has run away because of your love. But they say that a soldier who is in love, always wins the war," Dev said affectionately.

"Dev, stop tormenting me. *Tum toh phir shuru ho gaye*". I said.

"Hum to aap par khatm bhi ho jayenge. Now get ready we are going out," he laughed.

"Dev, I don't feel like going out." But when he insisted, I quickly got up and started getting ready. I had worn a yellow sari. On this sari, mummy had got beautiful Kashmiri embroidery done. Dev couldn't take his eyes off me.

"Will I keep on gazing at you only from a distance for the rest of my life? No, Mrinalini, *Ab yeh dooriyan nahin*"..., he said to himself.

Shubha did not accompany us, despite our insistence. We remained silent all the way.

The *gazal* kept playing in the car, *"Mausam aayenge jayenge, hum tumko bhul na paayenge."*

Last year in Allahabad, during summers I had sat down on the stairs of the officers' Mess when Dev had come to call me. He was humming.

"Jab garmi ke din aayenge

Tapti dopahrain laayenge

Sannatte shor machaayenge

Galiyom main dhool udaayenge

Patte peele ho jaayenge

Phool sabhi murjhaayenge

Hum tumko bhul na paayenge."

When I had got up holding his hand, my *duppatta* had got entangled in the cactus kept outside his room.

"These thorns always get hold of my *duppatta*."

"That's not true. Actually this cactus hold on to your *aanchal* out of love. In fact, just like me, they too cannot bear to be away from you. They don't want to let go of you. What I cannot express, they do so beautifully."

"Dev, I will miss you so much. These memories of yours, will keep me alive. Until then, I will re-live these past moments."

"Dev, please play some other *gazal*," I said, trying to make a conversation.

He then started to play one of Bashir Badr's *gazals*,

"Socha nahin, accha bura..."

"Mrinalini, I am playing your favourite *gazal*, can you smile now."

After a while we had reached the Sai Baba temple on Lodhi road. I went on to buy flowers. Otherwise on other occasion, I would say, "Dev give me money to buy *pooja ka saamaan.*" I had not asked for money this time nor had he teased me by saying, "Mrinalini, you spend so much. Here, take these 20 rupees."

He had told the flower seller to give me flowers and he handed over the *pooja thali* to me.

Dev had climbed the steps of the temple and stopped before Sai Baba and had said, "Mrinalini, I have always loved you and will continue to do so, even if there is a life beyond this. It's you who has been in my heart, in my thoughts, in my dreams, in my conscious and subconscious mind, and if there is anything beyond. Now, in the presence of God, let's vow to be together forever. Give your life and future to me and my dreams. Have faith in God, for He will always be merciful to us."

"Dev, you have always loved me so much and now you have turned our love into a beautiful relationship."

We both bowed down before Sai Baba.

Today, Dev had formalized our relationship. The fear of the norms and ways of the society which used to bother me had now become meaningless. My indecisiveness, I think was always very eager to lose out to his love, in fact, even this was a victory of sorts for us.

While returning, Dev had stopped the car near the bangle shop, "Darling, don't you want to buy some bangles?"

"Yes, I'll buy lots of them, Dev. Earlier, I never used to wear bangles or a *bindi*, neither *payals* nor *bichiyas*. I started wearing all these for you," I had said, resting my head on his back.

It felt very good wearing so many bangles in both my hands.

"And what *bindi* would you like to buy?"

"*Lal rang ki gol bindi*. Long ones only suit those who do not have a round face."

"The long *bindi* will look good on you even though you have a round face, for tomorrow when I will be gone you will sulk and make such a long face that it will anyway look good on your face," he had said teasing me.

"You tease me a lot, I am never going to talk to you again."

"Now say that I don't love you," he continued to tease me.

"Darling, *mehndi bhi lagwa lo*. Do you remember I had almost missed my flight while getting your hands adorned with *mehndi* last time? I had decided that if I was declared AWL* then I would tell my Commanding Officer, 'I was getting Mrinalini's hands adorned with *mehndi*'."

Then he said to the *mehndi waala*, "Make a beautiful design today on her hands and also on her feet."

---

* Away Without Leave

"Dev, what are you saying? Do you know how long will it take? How will I walk?"

"There is no need for you to walk I am here to carry you in my arms."

Everything is beautiful wherever there is love.

Wearing bangles in my *mehndi* adorned hands and becoming Mrs Dev Sharma was such a wonderful feeling.

"Dev I want to say so much, but I am unable to. There is so much to share with you."

I began to think that there is so much tranquility and peace in my life now. Now I look forward to tomorrow and I am confident that everything will be fine.

Dev has always been a big support in my life. He has always protected me. He has loved and accepted me along with my family—mummy, Shubha and Manu. I was never alone. He has always been with me. Manu had known only Dev as a father figure. It may be that a man would want to love such a woman who is single. He had always taken care of everyone.

Dev had stopped the car at the hotel. The receptionist had asked, "Are you just married? Congratulations!"

"Yes, we have just got married." Then he wrote in the register, Major and Mrs Dev Sharma.

While going up in the lift Dev had put his hand on my shoulder. He then had said softly, "So, you are mine and we are together forever. Mrinalini, I have waited for a lifetime for this moment to come. I wondered if this long wait would ever end? I would often console myself that may be one day you would say, 'Dev, please take me along.' In the last many years, we had hardly ever stayed together. We had been away from each other much longer than we had been together; but no *fauji* is ever able to stay with his wife for long."

He was very emotional and he continued, "Do you know for how many days we have been together—and the rest of the days and nights were spent in loneliness. When I was in Kashmir and spoke to you on a full moon night, I would look at the moon and think that you would also be looking at it, but we are so far away. Neither could you see me nor could I. But the moon that shines every night, is tonight here with me. Often while wandering in the jungles there, I would miss you. When I would return I would have many dreams but this loneliness would be my sole companion. I would then talk to myself. Your memories would brighten my dark nights. Why this silence, say something, Mrinalini?"

"Dev, you have always read my silence. Now listen to my silence and understand what I want to say. You came into my life and before I realized became a part of my existence. You alone are my past, my present and my future."

"Mrinalini, the whole world is mine if you are with me. Look at the setting sun, isn't it beautiful? For a long time I thought of you only as a friend. I did not realize exactly when I fell in love. One day, I realized that my existence is mcaningless without you. With you around everything become so beautiful. You always said that the most precious relationship has no name. But I always wanted to give a name to our relationship."

Saying this he became quiet. Perhaps he was thinking that, today my dream world has become a reality. He said, 'This belief will really bring me back to all my loved ones. In life only a certain amount of uncertainty is fine, but beyond this, there has to be a lasting stability. Mrinalini this uncertainty had become unbearable. No one can keep on going endlessly without wanting to reach a destination. To come back to you, I should know in which direction and how far I need to travel.'

"Dev, I don't know how I will treasure this love. Today destiny is smiling upon me."

"Mrinalini, I don't want to be a mere part of your life, but a part of you. I don't want few moments with you, but want to be with you for each day and each night. I want to be with you forever and ever."

He kept on looking lovingly at my *mehndi*-adorned hands, full of bangles. Many times he had held on to these beautiful hands in his dreams. Now, actually holding these hands, he was reminded of innumerable days that he had lived dreaming about them.

"Mrinalini, do you know when I first saw your beautiful feet, I just couldn't take my eyes off them. They were showing out of the *chadar* in that dimly lit train compartment. Thinking of them, many a times in my dreams I would find myself on that journey from Bangalore when I had met you for first."

Lost in our own world, we did not realize that it was morning already. Whenever Dev had to return after leave, I would become sad. "Once you will go back, mornings and evenings will become meaningless."

"Mrinalini, why do you fight and why do you cry? When you are unable to console yourself by crying, you start fighting with me. Will you be able to console yourself by fighting with me? Will you miss me less if your fight with me? Can you ever think of forgetting me? *Kya dhathura kha kar aayi ho?*" Whenever I fight with Dev, he always says this and I burst out laughing and the fight is over.

"Dev, its pointless to fight with you. Moments of love that I spent with you are very precious and I will live thinking of these moments."

"Darling, get up. Shubha must be waiting for us."

"*Yaar,* don't bring Shubha between us today. She is a very decent person. My morning has not begun as yet," Dev said lovingly.

"Dev please Let's go home. We must tell Shubha that we are married now."

"Darling, you are a *fauji's* wife. Stop being scared. Major Dev Sharma has married you. I want to sleep for some more time. I always wanted that I should someday go off to sleep and then get up in the morning and have you by my side. Okay, I am getting up now. Thank God, You are here with me."

"When the Unit was in Allahabad, I had become used to hearing your 'good morning' on the phone every morning at 5.30. When I was in Kashmir you could not call. I was unable to sleep then, because, you could not wake me up. Did you not see the pain in my eyes? I hadn't slept for weeks. I often console myself that someday you will be there besides me to wake me up. I will miss you so much it will be difficult for me to go back to the Unit alone, Mrs Sharma."

"Shall I inform your Commanding Officer that Major Dev Sharma is wounded, in love? He has been admitted in the home ICU." I said cajoling him to get up. Resting his head on my shoulder, he said, "Don't start sulking now. This is our first morning after getting married. Don't be upset. Fight with me if you want. I have surrendered totaling and unconditionally to you."

"Dev, what will we tell mummy? She may find it odd that we have got married in such a hurry."

"I have waited for five long years. We love each other. It was God who brought us together and it was the same Almighty who became a witness to our marriage. Have we come together just like that? God must have His reasons. So what is there to hide or to be scared of? Look back and what do you see? I can see endless dreams in your eyes. I have a dream which I am giving you today. *Faujis'* say "A man should love his woman a lot and understand her a little, whereas a woman should understand her man a lot and may be love him a little. So, Mrinalini, leave the love to me and start to understand me."

"You will be away for months. I don't know when you will come back. This upsets me and I worry a lot. I do not know what should I do? And to top it up you tease me."

"Why do you cry so much? Do you think I won't come back? Mrinalini, I promise, I will come back to you. When my loving wife and my sweet little Manu are waiting for me with such conviction, I have got to come back," saying this he took me in his arms.

"Dev, I will always cherish the beautiful dream that you are giving me. This dream would have turned into reality by the time you come back."

Then holding me in his arms, he said, "Do you remember once when I phoned, you were reading Dinkar's 'Urvashi'. You had read two lines and had asked me,—

"Kab tha aisa samay ki jab mera astitva nahin tha?
Kab aayega woh bhavishya jis din main nahin rahoongi?"

I had replied spontaneously, *"Jab main nahin tha, jab main nahin rahunga"*. Anyway, we are one. I exist because of you and you because of me how can we ever be apart."

I had become reflective that why Uday mama could not make such a promise with so much conviction to Jaya.

After a while, I said, "Dev, let's go now. Shubha will be waiting."

"I didn't ask earlier and didn't want to know also but I wonder why Shubha is still single?"

"Shubha is prettier than me and was very good at studies. Mummy did get a lot of proposals for her. But, perhaps she did not find the right person at the right time. I don't mean that she was unable to choose the right person but she just didn't come across such a person. She never makes her decisions in haste. Many guys wanted to marry her; she didn't find anyone of them suitable. I never tried to probe, for she is so dear to me. The day she decides to share something, I am there. Her classmate Sanjay Singh wanted to marry her. When he was leaving for the US, he again asked her to marry him. He kept on writing to her. They are still very good friends. I don't know why she refused his proposal. For a while we thought that she may relent, but mummy never pressurized her. The freedom that people give to their sons, mummy gave the same, to both of us. Mummy always insisted on good education. In our home education was never a means to prepare us for the marriage market."

I continued, Dev, Shubha says, "Whenever the right person comes along with whom I think I can spend my entire life, I will get married. I will never relent for marriage because of any pressure or compromise'."

"By the way Shubha is far more beautiful than you," Dev teased me.

"Ya, its true. As she has now become your sister-in-law she will appear far more prettier." I laughed.

I was suddenly reminded of my distant relative, Gita bua who always taunted mummy, "Bhabhi, has two-two daughters. Let's see how she will get them married after dada's death. On top these girls are studying more than what my sons have studied."

Gita bua even got some funny marriage proposal for the two of us. She would often say to mummy, "Bhabhi at least get rid of one of the girls quickly. What will you gain by educating then so much? They are not going to become a Collector any way. Get them married off and let them produce children. What else is needed of girls?"

Mummy would only laugh over her stupid advice,

"Bibiji, you are the only one who's worried about me. You are very fortunate to be the mother of two sons."

Anyway whenever buaji, would visit she would only leave after collecting innumerable gifts—sarees, sweets and even money. We all used to mock her behind her back. When she had come over a few months back, she appeared to be very unhappy and upset— "Bhabhi, my sons are new battling it out in the court. You are lucky to be a mother of two daughters, I wish I had just one such daughter."

"Darling, your buaji is a befitting example of 'better late than never'," he laughed.

"Shubha, has never regreted her decision of staying single. She says that she has had the pleasure of bringing up a child without getting into the hassles of marriage. She only has brought up Manu and Manu, too, is more attached to her."

"Manu addresses Shubha as mummy?" Dev asked.

"Dev, but for Shubha, I wouldn't have been able to get over the problems in my life. I had totally given up on life. I did not feel like speaking to anyone. I had completely lost myself. A baby has so many requirements—feeding, bathing, medicines and to keep awake in the nights whenever needed. I had become so negative that if I had cuddled the baby it would not have evoked any emotion. Shubha had bagged a very prestigious assignment in the US, but she did not take it up because she did not want to leave Manu, mummy and me. She took care of everything. I realized that my life was slowly coming back to normal. I started to feel that those carefree college days were back again," I kept on talking with my head in Dev's lap.

"I could overcome such a big crisis in my life only because of mummy and Shubha. They stood behind me like pillars of support. Mummy faced the innumerable questions of society, neighbours, relatives, but she kept me away from them. It's true that you are the one who finally pulled me out of it. Its your love and support that gave me the confidence that every day would bring something new and beautiful in my life."

We had kept on talking for a long time and did not realize that it was time for Dev to leave. For a moment it felt as if after giving us such togetherness, life had once again got us back to square one. Being together for a few days followed by long separation and endless waiting.

Dev was silent when Shubha did *tikka* as he was leaving. He only said, "Shubha, take of Mrinalini." He was absolutely quiet on the way to the airport. As we passed the Sai Mandir, I said, "Let's go to the mandir."

Dev got down and at the *phoolwaala's* shop handed over the wallet to me. When we started to climb the steps of the mandir, I kept on repeating to myself, 'God please, please bring back Dev safe, very soon. God, you have given me so much happiness now you only must secure it for me.'

We bowed before Sai Baba. The flowers given by the *pujari*, I put one in Dev's pocket and tied one to the corner of my *dupatta*. As always I put the garland around his neck, and then we left for the airport.

As we neared the airport, I don't know why I became so silent that Dev too could not bear it. He put his arm around me. Somehow I tried to control my tears and looked out of the window. I tried to console myself but failed miserably.

When we reached the airport, I could not bear it any longer. Putting my head on his shoulder I started crying.

"Dev, I will wait for you every moment. Come back home soon."

Then, controlling my tears with great difficulty, I barely managed to utter "Come back safe."

He handed over the garland to me saying, "Okay, see you darling," he started to move towards the departure gate.

I was right behind him. As he was about to enter, he said, "Mrinalini, keep writing to me...."

It was his habit, never to look back while going. I waited at the airport till the flight departed.

My feet felt like lead and it was difficult to take even a step. When I sat in the car, I remembered what Dev had said, "Mrinalini, why are you afraid of being alone? You have everyone—mummy, Shubha and Manu. Who knows, when I come back there may be someone else too, who will reiterate my presence in your life."

After two days when I sat down to write to him, I did not know what to write. I wrote whatever came to my mind.

Dearest Dev,

We wish for happiness in the times to come. We can pray to God. You did the correct thing by formalising our relationship. As for me I was living in such uncertainty. It was good that you were determined to give a name to our relationship; or else I would not have been able to do so because of my unknown fears. Being married is so beautiful. I acknowledge before you that Mrinalini without Dev is nothing. My life begins with you. The mere thought that you were ever to leave me scares me to death. You are now a part of my being. And this is what love is.

Dev, you would often ask me, "Mrinalini, what is that you want? What should I do that will make you happy?"

Dev, I do not know to this day what is it that I want, but I do know that all that I want, I want only from you. Dev, your eyes that look at me with love, your heart which sings for me, your soul and your love give all these to your Mrinalini. You would always compare my love to a meandering mountain river. Dev, I wish that you always keep flowing with it and then its for me to take you along wherever I wish. Will you not come along? Will you try to resist? But who has ever been able to resist flowing along with it? Just keep on going along with me for that is what I exist for. I am confident that no one will be able to hold back this river of love and no one will be able to diminish your love for that is what gives this river its flow.

I often remember watching the setting sun with you, getting drenched in the rain, and at night, you soulfully humming *'Mausam aayenge jayenge....'* I have forgotten nothing and never will. When I get upset because of being alone, its your dream that gives me solace like a shade in the searing sun.

Until you come home, life will be incomplete.

Yours,
Mrinalini

11

Slowly and steadily, life was coming back to its normal rhythm. I completely submerged myself in work.

Despite being so busy, I had ample time to think about Dev and the time we had spent together. However, Saturdays and Sundays were especially difficult to live by.

One day when I went shopping, I suddenly ran into Jaya aunty.

She asked lovingly, "How are you Mrinalini? And how is Dev?"

"Aunty, its been almost a month since Dev left. He had come on leave but was called back before the leave was over. We got married before he left. It was his decision or else left to myself, I would have not been able to decide anything."

"How wonderful! Congratulations! I pray to God that both of you are always together and remain happy. You are lucky to have found someone like Dev. He has given meaning to your life. This decision will bring immense happiness to both of you in the times to come. I am sure that he will come back soon. Your love will always bring him back to you. When I first met both of you, I know everything about Dev and you, without you having said anything. The future belongs to both of you and to your everlasting love."

Jaya aunty's eyes brimmed with tears. It appeared that the past was still bothering her and she could feel the pain of loss of Uday mama even now.

"Aunty, Dev took me to Sai mandir and he asked, "Mrinalini, listen to your heart before you decide about us." Good that he did that. Earlier, I had been unable to listen to my heart. We did meet for a number of times during the past years, but whenever I would return it felt as if I had left behind a part of myself with Dev and I could say yes."

"Mrinalini, you have everything even though Dev has gone back to Kashmir. I do not have Uday with me, what I have is an endless wait for the rest of my life. Everything changed for me when he did not come back home from the war. I cannot express my sorrow when he did not return. It felt as if life itself had become such a burden. As time passed, and all hopes of his return diminished. His memories are with me, for nothing ever remains, but memories," she had become very emotional.

"Aunty, after Uday mama did not return, each moment that mummy has lived waiting for him, I have lived with her. Mummy still hopes that may be, just maybe, some day he might come back home."

"Mrinalini, don't trouble yourself so much by thinking about Uday. Cherish and treasure Dev's love and the dreams he has given you. Slowly, this long wait will be over and before you realize, Dev will be back, just the way Uday had suddenly returned after liberating Goa. Don't associate our relationship because of Uday, instead think of it as a new relationship because our husbands are from the same Unit. Though my wait is endless, but Dev will definitely come back home very soon."

Be it the hot summer afternoon or the stillness of the nights; I would be lost in the happy times I had spent with Dev—sometimes oblivious to what was going around me. Many a times I would go to all those places where once we had been together. It appeared as if all these places were asking, "Why have you come alone?"

At times I would think about Uday mama and Jaya aunty and become very scared. I would then console myself that my Dev will come back to me very soon, he will have to.

After meeting Jaya aunty I tried to change my thought process that if Uday mama did not come back. Dev had promised that he will come back and he surely will.

Mummy would ask, "Mrinalini, tell me what is it that is bothering you? You appear so sad and tense for the last many days?"

I did not know how to answer this? How was I going to tell her that Dev and I had got married? Dev has gone back to Kashmir and when I do not hear from him, I get worried. But I couldn't say anything despite wanting to. Mummy still anxiously waited for Uday mama to return and what will happen if she were to know that now I was also waiting for Dev. I would be nearly in tears most of the times but took care to hide them from her.

One day I asked, "Mummy, when Uday mama did not come back…?" I put my head in her lap and started crying. I continued to sob, unable to say anything. Finally, gathering courage I said, "Dev has been recalled, that's why he could not meet you, mummy, I have no news of him since he left."

I managed to say this with difficulty but could not bring myself to say what will happen if Dev did not come back.

"Mrinalini beta, how will your worrying and crying help? If Dev realizes that you are so upset, he will get disturbed. It will be difficult for him to carry on with his work. Have confidence that he will come back. Stop getting upset because of Uday. If Uday did not return it does not mean that no one else will ever come back home to his loved ones. Think of those who have come back home from war."

Despite mummy's reassurances, I nearly choked when I said, "Mummy, I met Jaya aunty. She also said the same thing."

"Beta, I have been through such tough times—the loss of your nani, Uday, your papa and then nana I was sad, heartbroken, but life continued. I lived on for my children. When I look back and see, time flew and before I could realize Shubha and you had already grown up. Later, seeing you in difficulty, I was devastated. Was God always going to keep on testing me like this? Were there only struggles in my life? Then, I started to bring up Manu, and all my woes immediately vanished."

"Mummy, how will I get so much strength?" Until now, you have always shielded me from all troubles," saying this I started wondering how will I live through these days. Dev's memories kept haunting me. I tell myself that I will not re-live the torment that Jaya aunty had lived. But she had tried her best to tell me that Dev will definitely come back to me. I felt sad for her but I made a resolve not to compare her fate with mine.

"Beta, we all live our destinies but problems arise when we start reliving someone else's destiny. I still love Uday, he is a part of my life. But you should not live with the fear that destiny has the same in store for you, too. Always remember the love of Uday and Jaya. I don't know when exactly you started living this pain while sharing it with me."

Mummy tried her best to pacify me in her own way. Although while talking to her, I did feel relieved but I could not bring myself to tell her about my marriage to Dev. How worried she would be as there was a possibility of a war starting any time and one never knew what would happen the next moment.

Time moved on. I became busy with my work. I turned into a robot. But a corner in my heart would always think of Dev and wonder how would he be? Where would he be? When would he come back home?

Then at last, one day, Dev called, "How are you darling? Its raining here. I miss you a lot."

"Dev, it has been so long now, when will you come back home?"

"*Yaar,* do not cry like this. I will be tempted to abandon my post and run to you—*bhagode bana kar manogee kya?*" he did laugh but the underlying sadness could not be missed.

"I am fine, but why are you sounding so sad?"

"If you were to know that I will never come back, what will you do?" he had become emotional.

"What are you saying, Dev? What has happened today? Please, please, tell me? You had promised never to talk of such ominous things?" I was really tense and worried by now.

"When someone dear does not come back, how would one feel? Today Major Singh of our Unit,..." he wasn't able to go on.

"Major Singh, Oh! my God what happened?"

"He was to go on leave for his brother's wedding next week. One blast and everything was over in seconds."

I silently listened and thought that can a moment change so much?

"Mrinalini, what is life? One day, just like this everything is finished so quickly. What's *punya* and *paap*? Is there any reward for ones good deeds or a punishment for bad ones?"

"Dev, pull yourself up. I am with you. Then why do you speak like this?"

"Mrinalini, here a man's identity is a mere number. The moment you land up, your identity card is taken away and kept in safe custody. You are given a badge with a number which becomes your only identity."

"Dev, don't talk like this. Say something nice." Suddenly the exchange conked off.

The phone lines had been disconnected once again. The calls wouldn't go through. Towards the end of July, one day my call got through suddenly. Bimal was on duty at the PCO. Listening to his familiar voice I was overjoyed and asked, "Bimal, how is Major Sharma?"

"Mem saab, all is well. I will try and connect you to Sahab."

I don't know how but he connected my call to the post. Hearing Dev's voice I wasn't able to speak for a few moments.

Hearing his 'hello' for the second time, I said, "Dev, how are you and what are you doing?"

"I was obeying your command. I have given a name to these nameless rocks, I have just engraved your name on one of them."

"Really! How did you do that? Do you remember when and where I had asked you to engrave my name? How did you do it?"

"You had told me in Allahabad to write 'Mrinalini' on a rock in Kashmir. We had come back drenched in the rain. My dear, I remember whatever you say. I have engraved your name with a *khukhri*. With your kind permission, may I take up a little space besides it and engrave 'Dev', as well. Mrinalini, see you are even here with me. All these rocks were nameless but by engraving your name you are here with me in this wilderness."

"Dev, you have always loved me like mad."

I would very often remember the good times that we had spent together and would dream of a beautiful future ahead. I would be lost in my thoughts and one day my finger got crushed while closing the almirah. I was suddenly reminded of that day when my fingers were crushed when Dev had suddenly closed the car door. Three of my fingers had been badly bruised, and one of them had lost its nail. Dev was extremely upset, and he just sat there holding my injured hand. "Sorry, darling... what have I done?"

He had managed to get some ice in his hanky. "Mrinalini, it must hurt a lot. You are not even complaining.

"Dev, you have in fact, always shared the pain in my life. How can you ever hurt me?"

"Mrinalini, what a unique way of showing what I mean to you!"

He then insisted and took me to a doctor. When the doctor after bandaging my hand, handed over a bill for Rs. 120, I couldn't but laugh.

"What a waste of Rs. 120? We could have had a nice treat and some coffee too."

"You are crazy. Your fingers have been crushed so badly that it will take at least six months for the nail to grow again. And here you are, asking for a treat. Take care of your hand, otherwise it will keep on hurting. Come on now, tell me what treat do you want?"

I teased him and said, "Whatever you have given me with love is mine, even this injured hand. I want to have ice-crème. The doctor has done a bad job with the dressing and its hurting even more now."

I also remembered when once Dev had returned a few days late from exercise I had got very angry. I had not spoken to him for days. He had his own special way of making up. He always said that love and madness go hand-in-hand.

"I will always continue to love and will never let you remain upset with me."

"How are you going to make up for this? I am not going to relent this time."

"Mrinalini, *tum jitni baar roothogi utni baar manaunga*. Any doubts?"

"Pyaar mein kitni baar naak ragdoge meri naak par. If I don't relent even after a 100 counts what will you do?"

"101, 102, ... till you yield. I even cherish small bits of your love. Unless you smile even destiny will not smile on me."

These memories of Dev were my only solace those days but each day was difficult to live without him.

Earlier, whenever I used to clean and rearrange his room, he would get irritated, "Mrinalini, come here and talk to me. Why are you wasting these precious moments in cleaning and decorating the room?"

"The room has become so dirty. Why don't you go out and buy some plants, meanwhile let me do up the room."

When he would return and see the nicely done up room, he would become sad. "Who will do all this for me? I will miss you even more."

"Shall I stay back for another day?" I would ask him lovingly.

"Mrinalini, stay back for ever. Don't ever go back." He would always say.

He would lie down with his head in my lap and say, "Mrinalini, talk to me. Am I destined to be always alone?"

"Dev, don't say that." I would take him in my arms.

Days would start and end. Nights would also fall and end. Earlier when he was around I would cry on his shoulder. But now, the sleepless nights had taken away that comfort. When I would try to write a letter my mind would go blank.

Many a times I had sent a blank paper in an envelope to him. The times we had happily spent together were like a mirror before me. In the morning while having tea with mummy in the garden, I was always reminded of Dev sipping tea in the lawns of the Mess.

"Mrinalini, this sun has brought our shadows so close together."

"I can only see you Dev, and a shadow."

"Mrinalini, then where are you."

"Dev, you are there along with your shadow, which is me. I have no other existence now, apart from you."

October came, and I fell ill. A long bout of high fever had completely drained me. Mummy and Manu had been with Shubha for some time now. Mummy came back as I was battling with my illness all alone.

"Mrinalini, what is this? Take care of yourself. This depression will land you in hospital very soon," she admonish me. But I kept quiet.

She enquired again, "It's nearly four months now. Are you aware of what is bothering you? Unless you know of it, no one can help you. What is it? Go on...tell me."

"Mummy, you think that Dev and I are only good friends, but the truth is that we have got married. When we had gone to IMA and RIMC in May, was when his leave was cancelled and he was recalled. When we returned to Delhi, we decided to get married. When I do not get any news of him, I get worried. Mummy, I... has Dev told you anything?"

"Dev had said to me much earlier, 'Aunty, take care of Mrinalini. Just because Capt Uday Sharma did not return does not mean that I too will not come back. I don't know how she is going to survive like this? Before returning to Kashmir, we had got married. My wife remains distraught thinking of Capt Uday Sharma and Jaya ma'am.'"

"Mummy, that day when I was speaking to you and crying, you did not mention that you knew about our marriage."

"When children have grown up it's up to them to inform their elders about important decisions they take. It would not have been proper on my part to be inquisitive. Mrinalini, did you think – what will mummy think? If you had to take such a decision amidst the great uncertainty of war, I see nothing wrong in it. A decision taken after much thought and deliberation is not necessarily always the right decision."

Towards October end came *Karwa Chauth*. I was unwell and on top of it, I had not taken leave because I wanted to save my leave for when Dev would come home.

"Mrinalini, you are such a *kanjoos* as far as taking leave goes. Even when you are unwell, or there is dire need, you never take leave." Dev would often crib.

That afternoon Dev called. "How are you, darling?"

"I am okay," I said in a subdued voice.

"Why are you crying? I am so happy here. Yesterday few of my course mates had come over and I gave them a treat for our marriage."

"Here, I am fasting for you without any food or water. There you are throwing parties for people. You are never so generous with me."

"Where shall I treat you and to what? My heart is full of generosity for you. But do I still have it with me? Someone has already stolen it. God bless her. By the way why are you fasting?"

"It's *Karwa Chauth*. I am fasting without food and water. You never remember anything."

"Mrinalini, without you day and night, weeks and months, all feel the same. Time just goes by. I keep re-living the memories of those days of roaming the streets of Chandni Chowk in Delhi or the Civil Lines in Allahabad with you."

After fasting the whole day, by evening I was totally drained and had collapsed on the bed. Shubha had come down from Delhi and it was she who made all the preparations for the *puja*. After the *puja*, when I at last gulped some water, I could barely open my eyes. Shubha called out affectionately, "Mrinalini," and I burst out crying. She was perhaps aware of my condition.

"Mrinalini, have you seen a doctor? Mummy has gone to Kanpur for a wedding and she has told me to take care of you."

"What will the doctor do? I am fine. Don't worry about me."

"Is Dev aware of your condition? Have you told him?"

"Please, don't say anything to him."

"Look, if Dev does not come back soon, I will have to tell him that you are not well. I will also tell him that you will be in this condition for some time," she laughed.

"Have you guessed?"

"So what if I haven't got married? I can certainly guess the reason for your condition. We will see a doctor tomorrow."

By November, it was certain that Dev would be coming home. He was to travel to Delhi from Srinagar. The flight was scheduled for 3 p.m. Shubha was busy so I went alone to receive him. I had become tired of waiting. I hadn't eaten anything since morning. It felt as if would faint. The flight finally landed after a long wait. Seeing Dev walk towards me, gave me immense joy. I leaned on the railing. He walked towards me, smiling and waving.

"I am here then why this love for the railing?" he extended his hand and I fell in his embrace.

"Darling what is it? You are looking so pale and exhausted. You got tired of waiting for me? Was the wait so long? Where is Shubha? Where is my sweet little Manu? I missed everyone a lot. But why have you come alone? Are you upset with me? Come, let's have coffee."

Again, so many question at one go. This was so much like Dev.

"Why are you sulking? I have come back. Will you still show love in bits? Are you angry with me for some reason?"

"I am not angry, Dev. I am simply not well."

"What's happened? You don't eat properly, and to top it, so many fasts. Do you think I will be safe if you go without food and water? When I go back, I will have to appoint somebody who will make sure that you eat well, and report back to me. Are you upset because you had to come alone?" he laughed.

"I have not come alone, Dev." I smiled.

"But where is Shubha then?"

"Shubha has not come, but someone else has."

He held me by my shoulders and started looking around. Then he gestured and asked as to who was it that had come with me.

"Someone who has always been with me ever since you left." I put my head on his shoulder.

"Really? Why didn't you tell me before! Has my wife started to love someone more than me? Had I known, I would have felt happy that you are not alone any longer. I was unnecessarily worried that you were waiting for me to return, all by yourself. Who knew that now many people were waiting for me? Manu, you and someone new!" He was delighted and hugged me lovingly.

"I love you so much, my darling. Look at the dreams I have in my eyes. Now that so many good things are happening one after the other, life seems so wonderful. It's a great feeling."

Then humming, *"Mausam aayenge, jayenge..."* he walked out of the airport with his arm around me.

AND...

Uday and Jaya had loved each other. Dev loves his Mrinalini deeply, and that's why I could tell their story. I complete this story with a hope that every Dev in this world will always come back home to his Mrinalini. He will have to.

This is not the end, but the beginning of their endless love.

Let Uday's not coming back home be an exception. I wish that it remains the sole exception, and that every Uday comes back home to his Jaya... Always.